"An adopted son…" Jo echoed. Not an old girlfriend after all, but a child.

"He's not legally mine yet," Alex said, "but it won't be long now. He's an orphan and we just… connected. Like you and me, you know?"

Jo stood and moved away from him. She needed room to take this in. Had they "just connected"? That wasn't how she remembered it.

"Look, I realize it's kind of a shock," he went on, "and the timing could be better, but I know you'll love him as much as I do."

"Tell me one thing, Alex. What would be better timing?"

"I wanted to have this night, just for us, without complications. I didn't want to spring my son on you like this. Not before…before…"

"We slept together?"

Dear Reader,

This month, Silhouette Romance has an exciting lineup for you—perfect reading for these warm, romantic summer nights—starting with a new BUNDLES OF JOY title from Kristin Morgan. In *Make Room for Baby,* a new arrival brings Camille Boudreaux and Bram Delcambre together as a family—and gives their lost love a second chance.

Stella Bagwell brings her heartwarming style to the FABULOUS FATHERS series with *Daddy Lessons.* Joe McCann was about to fire Savanna Starr until he saw her skill at child rearing. But would helping this single dad raise his teenage daughter lead to a new job—as his wife?

Another irresistible cowboy meets his match in the latest WRANGLERS & LACE title, *Wildcat Wedding.* Look for this tale of Western loving by Patricia Thayer.

As for the rest of the month, you'll be SPELLBOUND by Sandra Paul's humorous tale of a very determined angel and the very stubborn bachelor she tries to reform in *His Accidental Angel.* Charlotte Moore brings a *Belated Bride* back to her hometown to face the man who left her at the altar. And Judith Janeway makes her debut this month with a charming and humorous love story, *A Convenient Arrangement.*

Happy Reading!

Anne Canadeo
Senior Editor

Please address questions and book requests to:
Silhouette Reader Service
U.S.: 3010 Walden Ave., P.O. Box 1325, Buffalo, NY 14269
Canadian: P.O. Box 609, Fort Erie, Ont. L2A 5X3

A CONVENIENT ARRANGEMENT

Judith Janeway

Silhouette
R O M A N C E™
Published by Silhouette Books
America's Publisher of Contemporary Romance

To Bob, my own true love,
and
to the Sisters of the Pen,
with thanks for all you taught me.

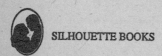 SILHOUETTE BOOKS

ISBN 0-373-19089-1

A CONVENIENT ARRANGEMENT

Copyright © 1995 by Judith Wrubel

JUDITH JANEWAY

began her career as a published author at age ten when she won an essay contest run by her local newspaper. She enjoys a challenging career as a writer, researcher and lecturer in health psychology, but she also has never abandoned her lifelong dream of writing romance fiction.

She and her husband, who shares her dreams, live in Northern California with their three children. When asked what she does in her spare time, she usually responds, "What's spare time?"

OREGON

CALIFORNIA

NEVADA

• San Francisco

• Monterey

• Santa Barbara

Santa Barbara Islands

• Vista del Mar
• Los Angeles

PACIFIC OCEAN

• San Diego

MEXICO

All underlined places are fictitious.

Prologue

"Don't cry, son. Daddy will be back for you." Alex MacHail pulled his crutches from under his arms and sank onto the side of the hospital bed, careful not to bump Buddy's foot. He reached out to the small face on the pillow and brushed the tears from the child's cheeks with his fingers.

"Don't go, Daddy," Buddy said, tears welling up in his brown eyes again.

Alex swallowed hard, trying to get rid of the perpetual lump in his throat. It hit him like a ton of bricks every time Buddy called him Daddy.

Buddy grabbed his hand with both of his small ones. "Don't go."

"I must go home, back to the *Estados Unidos,*" Alex said, patiently repeating what he'd said over and over for the past week. "So I can get *el permiso* to adopt you and bring you home. *¿Comprende?*"

Buddy blinked hard and nodded.

What a champ. Only four, but he'd faced pain and loss with more courage than a lot of grown-ups Alex could think of, including himself. Hell, he'd been so full of self-pity when he'd met Buddy, he'd even bought all the doctors' worst prognoses. He'd thought he'd never get his leg back a hundred percent, never act again.

"Remember when I first met you?" Alex asked.

Buddy nodded, a smile starting to show.

"And you said, *'Me llamo Alejandro.'* And I said, 'Me, too, my name is Alejandro'?"

"Now I am call Buddy," he said in gently accented English.

"That's right. But that's just a nickname," Alex said. "Our real names are the same. Not only that, we have the same hurt foot." Alex pointed to the cast on his right leg.

"Not same. My foot," Buddy said, pointing to the thickness of the cast that showed through the thin blanket covering him. "Your..." He squinted his eyes with the effort of trying to think of the word in English. *"¿Cómo se dice pierna?"*

"Leg," Alex supplied.

"Your leg," Buddy said with emphasis.

Alex shrugged in dismissal. "Same difference," he said, and swallowed again. He had a hard time with this part, because the difference had been so much more than foot and leg. He'd had a chance to live out his dreams, right up to a costarring role in two films, before a set had collapsed on him, shattering his hopes along with his leg. But what chance had Buddy ever had, an orphan with a deformed foot?

"Do you remember what else we found out? How else we're alike?" Alex asked.

Buddy's eyes grew wider, and his smile spread across his face.

"We found out," Alex went on, "that you didn't have a daddy and I didn't have a little boy. And you said..."

"'I be your little boy,'" Buddy crowed happily. "And you said, 'That best...'" He paused, frowning, clearly trying to remember the unfamiliar words.

"'That's the best offer I've had all day,'" Alex finished for him. And he'd meant it. A crazy idea, everyone said—

it's very hard to adopt as a single father, you don't even have a job right now, do you know anything about Mexican adoption laws and what about your leg? But this gutsy little kid had already walked into his heart and taken over.

Buddy still clung to his hand. Alex leaned forward. "Give me a kiss." Buddy circled his neck with his arms and kissed him on the cheek. Alex cradled the boy's head between his hands and gazed into his trusting eyes.

"Don't forget, you have the map." He gestured with his head to the map taped to the wall, a straight line inked in from Mexico City to Los Angeles. "And you have the calendar. I've marked the day I'm coming back to see you. You cross off each day and you'll know when you'll see me next."

"And then I go home?"

Alex winced. This hurt more than a compound fracture. But he couldn't lie. "No. Not then. It'll take a long time before I can bring you with me. But I'll visit you as often as I can. Remember I told you that?"

Buddy nodded, his eyes glistening. "*Sí,* I remember."

Alex gave him one last hug. He had to get out of there before he lost it altogether. He sat up and grabbed his crutches. Two nurses hovered outside the door, waiting to see how Buddy was going to take his departure.

He hoisted himself awkwardly off the bed and onto his crutches, making a funny face at Buddy over his clumsiness. Buddy blinked away his tears and smiled at him. The nurses didn't have anything to worry about there. His kid had grit enough for two. Now, *he* was another story.

He gripped his crutches. If Buddy could handle it, so could he. He'd get his leg back one hundred percent. And he'd get good roles again. He'd show them he could support a child. He moved to the doorway, then turned back for one last look. Buddy gazed back solemnly at him. He seemed so small in the big bed.

"Don't forget. I'll be back soon. *Te amo, mi hijo.*"

"*Te amo, papi.*"

Chapter One

The instant Jo stepped through the conference-room door she saw the problem—six feet and some to spare of sculpted good looks. Take as given the hot-air-balloon ego, because he was unquestionably an actor. And he was wrong, completely wrong, for the part. If Ron had already cast him, he meant weeks of work down the drain. She would have to rewrite the entire script.

"Jo, come in and meet Alex," Ron announced unnecessarily, since she was already in the room. She took a quick glance around. The four of them stood to one side of the long table—the actor, Ron and Ron's two accomplices. The head writer and the casting director both avoided her gaze—Bea chain-smoking and Cathy very interested in the state of her cuticles. Jo leaned back against the doorjamb and folded her arms across her chest.

"This is Alex MacHail. He's going to be playing the role of Johnny," Ron boomed. "Alex, this is Jo Barnett, writer *extraordinaire*. She is one of the people who keeps 'The Triumph of Love' in the top ratings day after day, week after week."

Yeah, right. He must have been rehearsing that introduction since breakfast, the big phony. What a way to tell her he'd dropped her mixed-race love story. She stayed at her post by the door.

Alex MacHail smiled in her direction. It didn't hurt his looks at all. Well, she was in no mood for hand shaking or making nice. Forget the laser blue eyes. He was an actor, and she'd learned about actors the hard way. She didn't smile back. "Jo's team has written your character's story line," Ron explained to Alex.

"No, we haven't," Jo corrected him. "We wrote a story line this actor is not suited for."

Ron waved his hand in a dismissive gesture. "Naturally, it will take a little bit of rewriting."

"A *little* bit!"

"Since the Johnny story line was your idea—" Ron spoke slowly like a parent whose patience was wearing thin "—I thought you could give Alex a handle on what's going down."

Why did he, a man who thought a mixed metaphor was a cocktail, talk to her as if she were a three-year-old? She jabbed a finger in his direction. "You gave me your word. I do not do evil twins, amnesiacs, or reappearances of presumed-dead husbands and wives. But you said, 'You're my most productive writer, Jo. I'll never ask you again, Jo. Write the evil twin story line for me and you can have any sensitive subject you want except cross-dressing.'"

"You have to consider the audience. Viewer polls show—"

"Get real," Jo interrupted.

"You want real? Real is our advertisers don't like it," Ron said. "They think Alex is right for the show. Cathy was lucky to get him for the part, and we're excited about the possibilities."

As far as she could see, they looked anything but excited. Bea continued to chain-smoke. Cathy had moved from cuticle inspection to picking at invisible lint on her suit.

Ron leaned on the back of a chair and glared aggressively at Jo. She stood, arms crossed, and stared right back. Alex MacHail looked back and forth at them like a spectator at a slightly boring tennis match.

"Can I be let in on the problem?" he asked. His voice had a pleasant kind of rasp to it. It went without saying that he'd have a voice to match those eyes and cheekbones.

"You're the wrong color," Jo snapped.

"What color was I supposed to be?" Alex asked.

"Black."

"I see." The beginnings of a smile crinkled the corners of his eyes. "Well, I'm good, but I can't do black."

Just what they needed, an actor who did stand-up. She pushed away from the doorjamb.

"Sorry, I'm too busy to exchange one-liners. I have a rewrite to do. Unless you've changed your mind about taking the role?"

"Know what?" He fixed her with his blazing blue gaze. Laughter showed behind his eyes, and something else, too. "I just realized how much I'm looking forward to it."

Jo whipped out of the room and strode down the hall to the warren of little offices where the writers worked. Didn't these actors realize how pathetic they were? As if she would fall down at his feet simply because he smiled at her. She threw open the door of Fran's office and found her co-writers, Fran and Ed, waiting for her.

"Want to know why Ron had to see me in the conference room in such an ASAPing hurry?" she stormed. "Because he's cast the Johnny role with a white actor, that's why."

She slumped into the third chair in the office across from her two co-workers. "Is he a slimy liar or what? Why did I believe him when he said we could have the Johnny story line if I filled in for Dorothy?" She looked at them with narrowed eyes. "Why do I have the feeling that none of this is news to you?"

"Because we hotfooted it right down to Linda the Living Listening Device and asked, that's why," Fran replied with a smug toss of her red hair.

"That reminds me," Ed interjected, a grin spreading across his thin face. "How are Linda and cable TV alike?"

Jo and Fran both groaned.

"Why groans? You haven't heard the punch line," he protested, then plowed ahead. "Because they both get good reception. Get it? A receptionist who gets good reception."

"We're going to have to impose sanctions, Ed," Jo warned. "We agreed to drop the Alike Game."

"That was funny, Ed," Fran said. "But we did vote. Two to one."

"Besides, this is serious," Jo said. "Our Johnny script is dead. Six weeks of work down the drain. And me doing double duty covering for Dorothy. If she hadn't gotten sick, I never would have been tricked into making that deal with Ron."

"Speaking of Dorothy," Fran said, "she's getting out of the hospital today."

"Great. I'm going to tell her the next time she decides to have her gall bladder removed, she'd better have an evil-twin script already written and waiting in her file drawer," Jo said.

"She asked me to take her home, so you two start the new script without me if I'm not here," Fran said.

"Thanks a lot," Jo said. "I have the perfect story idea already. How about an evil twin with amnesia who everyone thought was dead?"

"That should be noncontroversial enough for Ron," Fran said with a smile.

"Amazing. The man has four Emmys and still doesn't know that controversy makes for high ratings," Ed observed.

"Ron is not a risk taker. This time he wants to go with a sure thing. So we're stuck with Mr. Alex MacHail," Jo put in.

"You met him? What's he like?" Fran asked.

Jo gave an extravagant flourish of her hand. "Oh, dahling, he's simply perfect. He'll be *so* convincing as a young, streetwise tough guy who's been on his own since age sixteen. Late twenties, incredible blue eyes, cheekbones out to here, a jaw designed by Michelangelo, upper lip just a teensy bit larger than the lower lip and a hint of an overbite—very sexy. We'll have to be sure to have lots of scenes with him in a tank top, or better yet, stripped to the waist. I'm sure there are some impressive pecs under his Giorgio Armani.''

"Actually, they're not impressive, but they are respectable.'' The soft rasp came from the open door behind her. Jo swiveled her chair around slowly. Alex MacHail stood there, smiling slightly, hands in his pants pockets.

Funny, but she wasn't embarrassed, more pleased with herself, really. Besides, it was probably time he found out that not all women found him irresistible.

Cathy who was standing behind him, darted her gaze rapidly from Fran to Ed. "I'm taking Alex on a tour. I thought the whole team would like to meet him before we go downstairs.''

Ed was instantly on his feet, right hand outstretched. "Ed Selkin.'' He gestured with his left hand. "This is Fran Marcus.''

Alex shook Ed's hand, then Fran's. "Nice to meet you.''

"Hello again.'' Jo waggled her fingers at him in greeting and smiled her most phony polite smile. Alex gave back his nice grin, the one that started with the eyes crinkling. There was something intimate about the way he looked at her, as if they were sharing a private joke. Jo shifted uneasily in her chair.

"You all work in this one office?'' Alex asked, still in the doorway. He could enter no farther.

The room did look ridiculously jam-packed, Jo admitted. There was only room enough for the three office chairs, one desk, a computer and a printer.

"Well, we call it work,'' she answered. "Everybody else around here calls it fooling around or wasting time.''

"We do each have a separate office,'' Fran added hastily, "but part of the time we need to work together. We use my office for that because—''

"Because of boisterousness," Ed finished for her. "My office is on that side." He jerked his thumb to the right. "Jo's on the other to baffle the noise. Fewer complaints that way."

"I always thought writing was quiet work," Alex said.

"Discussions before writing get noisy," Ed explained. "Fran's a quiet writer. Me, too. Just little click, click, clicks on the word processor. Our little prodigy—" Ed gestured toward Jo "—writes on the piano. Makes her immune to writer's block."

Alex raised a questioning eyebrow.

"I play the piano in between bouts of writing," Jo told him. "It helps me not to think." She bit her lip. Why had she said that? She didn't have to explain herself to him.

"You have a piano in your office?" he asked.

"No. At home. We all do a lot of work at home." She didn't have time for this. He already had the part—what else did he want from them?

Then she noticed his hair—long brown hair drawn back and secured at the nape of his neck. It wouldn't do. Just like the rest of him, it wouldn't do at all.

"By the way, the long hair is going to have to go. I don't know what we're going to make of this character you're supposed to be, but even if he had long hair it would at least be cut in some style."

"Sorry, but the hair has to stay for now. It's in my contract." He didn't look sorry at all, more like slightly amused.

"You put your hair length in your contract? Who do you think you are, Samson?"

"Don't mind her, Alex," Ed interjected. "She got up on the wrong side of her high horse this morning."

"Yes, but that was a bed of a different color," she said. Then they both turned and waited for Fran.

Fran gave them her wide-eyed, innocent look. "Well, you've made your horse, now you've got to sleep on it," she said.

They turned back to the two standing in the doorway.

"Don't mind us," Ed said. "We just needed a brief break to play a game of, of..." He hesitated. "What were we playing?"

"How about Addled Adages?" Jo offered.

"Addled Adages it is," Ed declared. "Okay, please tell us about your hair. We're dying to know."

"If Jo had stayed at the meeting long enough I would have been able to explain," Cathy said testily. "He still has to finish shooting a Western for Pavilion Pictures. They asked us not to mess with his hair."

"You know, I'm sure our hairstylists could come up with a solution," Fran said. She turned to Alex. "They are very creative about this kind of thing."

"Okay," Cathy agreed, "we'll stop by when we go downstairs, but what do I tell them we're looking for?"

Jo, Fran and Ed looked at one another for a long moment. "That," Jo finally answered, "is the to be or not to be."

"Huh?" Cathy asked.

"The question," said Alex. "It's a quote from *Hamlet*. 'To be or not to be, that is the question.' Right?" He turned an engaging smile on the three seated writers.

"Hey, guys," Jo said. "The new kid wants to know if he can play too."

"Is that one of your games, like Addled Adages?" Alex asked, unperturbed.

"Jo was regressing," Ed replied. "That was Queer Quotations. Addled Adages is the exciting game of the moment."

"It wasn't Queer Quotations. It was Singular Citations," Fran put in.

"Please!" Cathy said through clenched teeth. "What am I supposed to tell the hairstylist?"

"How should we know?" Jo came right back at her. "We're good, but we can't do instant scripts." She saw Alex grin in recognition of his own line and hurried on. "Tell her 'tough.'"

"That's it? Tough?" Cathy asked.

"Yes. Tough. Generic tough. We'll fill in the blanks later."

Jo slumped farther down in her chair while the others said their nice-to-meet-you's. Then Fran leaned forward in her seat and peered at Alex's departing back. "Is he limping?" she asked.

She got up and went to stand in the doorway to watch. Ed joined her. "You may be right," he said.

"So what?" Jo mumbled. "He probably got a blister playing tennis."

"Jo, you're not paying attention." It was his serious tone. Jo paid attention. "Come over here. This may be an angle for the new script. *Johnny* has a limp."

Alex leaned against the wall by the elevators. Blast this leg to hell. It was fine yesterday, but today it had to stiffen up. The pain was no big deal. He was used to that by now. But what if it cost him the part? U.S. immigration wanted proof of full employment before they'd issue a visa for Alejandro. That talk about contracts had been half bluff—the show hadn't signed him on yet.

He saw Cathy watching him, her brow wrinkled in a little frown. It was time to head off the hovering concern, the curiosity, the invitation to sit down and rest his leg.

"That was one tough casting call," he told her with a grin. Cathy clearly didn't care much for the writers' brand of humor. He'd had fun, though, teasing that little fire-eater, Jo.

"They're always like that," Cathy said with a dismissive wrinkle of her nose. "Don't take anything Jo says personally. She's been off men since she got dumped."

So that was it. Some men didn't know when they were well off. All the better for him, though, because he was definitely interested.

"Is that so?" he replied, making it a question to encourage confidences.

Cathy leaned closer and lowered her voice. "She had a thing with a guy on the show. He went to Aspen alone and came back with Misty Davis. You know, the cover model. Jo took it pretty hard, I guess. Sort of has it in for the opposite sex.''

Jo didn't seem to have it in for Ed Selkin, though. Alex was about to say so when Ed himself called down the hall.

"Hey, Alex. Could you come back here a moment? There's something we want to ask you."

Alex walked toward the office, trying not to limp. Cathy trailed behind him. All three writers were crowded into the doorway scrutinizing him.

When he reached them, Ed said directly, "You have a limp."

No point in denying it. Had they found the excuse they needed to refuse him the part? He caught Jo peering at him as if he were a specimen under a microscope. This was not the way he wanted to get her attention.

He looked directly at her, and she quickly looked away. It was the darnedest thing—the way every thought showed on her face. Just a flash of embarrassment before she blinked her eyes and shifted her gaze.

He leaned his shoulder against the doorjamb and shifted his weight completely to his good leg. He wasn't going to say anything. If they wanted the sordid details, let them ask.

"There was an accident on the set of the picture," Cathy said, filling the silence. "Several people were injured and Alex broke his leg. He's fine now. The limp is temporary. Right, Alex?"

Alex nodded.

"But one of the other principals is still recuperating," she went on. "That's why they've had to delay finishing the film."

The three writers seemed not to be listening to her explanation. They moved back into Fran's office and took the same seats as before. Fran opened a notepad on her knee and began doodling. Jo did silent left-handed piano exercises, using the desktop as a keyboard. Ed put his hands behind his head, leaned back in his chair and consulted the ceiling.

"Okay," Ed began, "we have a tough guy with a limp."
There was a silence while they all thought this over.

"It happened when he was a child," Fran said slowly,
'and that's why he was taken away from his mother and put
n a foster home."

"His mother's boyfriend physically abused him." Jo
icked up the thread of the story they were weaving. "He
vas taken away from his mother and grew up in a foster
ome, had a rough time and became a real tough guy."

"He does bodybuilding so no one will mess with him. No
ne will think he's weak," Ed went on.

"But he's never forgiven his mother for letting him get
rippled," Fran added. "Now he's an adult and Lorna goes
o search for him for his mother's sake, so she can get his
orgiveness before she dies."

"And that is going to be a three-hankie forgiveness scene,
ny friends," Ed said with a grin.

"Wait, let's try this angle," Jo said, her fingers still play-
ng on an imaginary keyboard. "He thinks his mother
loesn't love him because he's crippled. Actually, she felt so
guilty she couldn't handle it. She does love him and can't
orgive herself. But he spends his whole childhood thinking
ne's unattractive and unlovable.

"Think about it." She let her hands drop to her lap and
wiveled her chair around to face Alex and Cathy standing
n the doorway. "Given that Johnny has a face and body
ike that, how likely is it that he will have trouble accepting
hat Lorna loves him? He has to have no idea how good-
ooking he is, or Lorna can't do her social work on him."

Every time she said he was good-looking she made it
sound like a defect. But he had the part. Relief seeped
through him. He'd call the adoption agency this afternoon
and see if they couldn't speed things up.

"So keep up the respectability of those pecs. And don't
forget how to limp," Jo said to him abruptly.

"No, ma'am, I won't," he said in his best Western drawl.
She couldn't dislike him all that much, could she?

"So I take it that now you know more about the characte ter?" Cathy asked. "Do I tell Gloria something other tha 'generic tough'?"

"Well, you heard us. Unattractive tough, if that's at a possible in this case." Jo flicked a glance at Alex. "Toug because he has low self-esteem, defensive, a real chip on h shoulder."

Cathy edged away from the door. Alex stayed for one la comment.

"You really do work as a team. I can't believe ho quickly you put that together."

"Well, you know," Jo quipped. "Necessity is the child o invention."

"That's right," Fran added. "Like son, like mother."

Alex couldn't resist. "Well, I guess necessity knows best. It was worth it. Jo's brown eyes sparkled, laughed right int his, for just an instant. Then she must have remembere herself.

"Ed, the new kid just stepped all over your lines. Aren' you going to defend your honor?" Jo challenged.

Ed clutched at his shirtfront. "Ooh, it's my angina Quick, my pills."

Jo threw a pencil at him.

Fran swatted him on the knee with her pad of paper. "E Selkin. You are such a bad loser."

"Ignore him," Jo said to Alex and Cathy. "He alway tries something when he loses."

"We really should get going, Alex," Cathy said.

He glanced at Cathy. "Okay, sure." He looked back a Jo. "See you," he said.

Jo waited until Alex and Cathy had walked off, then sh muttered, "Not if I see you first." She gave the door a pus with the tip of her shoe and waited for it to click shut. The she turned her chair to face her friends.

"I thought Alex was very nice. Didn't you, Ed?" Fra asked.

Ed nodded amiably.

"He certainly was taken with you, Jo," Fran went on.

"Puh-leeze, Fran." Jo rolled her eyes exaggeratedly.

"I don't want to sound like a broken record," Fran said, "but don't you think dating other men would help you get over Nick?"

"And I don't want to sound like a cracked CD, but I am not only over, I am done with, finished, ended, concluded, terminated..."

The ringing of the phone cut Jo off. Fran quickly picked up the receiver.

"Fran here... You're ready? Okay, I'll be right there." She hung up the phone. "That was Dorothy," Fran explained. "I doubt if I'll be gone long. She has another friend who's going to come and look in on her." Fran grabbed her purse and headed for the door. "Be good, you two," she warned as she went out.

"We will," Jo said. The door closed. "Not," she added. She turned to Ed and grinned. "Did you see what I sent you on E-mail this morning?"

Ed spun his chair around, punched a few keys on the computer, then peered at the screen. " 'The Nick Keith Memorial Landfill,' " he read, " 'has been established in recognition of a lifetime of scurrilous behavior. Bring all your nonrecyclable refuse to his home—see address below—to honor this great achievement.' " He turned to Jo. "Terrific. I love it. What should we do, set it up as a poster or send it out on E-mail?"

"Neither," Jo replied quickly. "This is for your eyes only. Don't show it to Fran."

A doubtful frown creased Ed's brow. "Why?"

Jo swiveled her chair restlessly from side to side. "You heard her. She keeps saying I've got to get over Nick. Last week she even said that I had to 'let go of my anger.' I told her she'd been reading too many self-help books."

Ed straightened in his seat. "Hold everything. That's not a fair call," he said. "Fran's not one to psychobabble at you. She only wanted to help, I'm sure."

Jo abruptly halted her restless chair-turning. There was a strange tone to Ed's voice, very defensive.

And that was a very dopey look on his face. A glimmer of an idea came to her.

"By any chance," Jo said, dragging out the words "could it be, is it possible, that you have a *thing* for Fran?"

Ed looked out the window. The view of the parking lot must have been compelling. He didn't answer her.

"Eh-ed!" She made his name a two-syllable word.

Ed turned away from the window. "Is Crumb-bum Construction still trying to force you out of your apartment?"

Jo leaned back in her chair and tapped her fingers on the armrests. "It's Cranshaw Construction. The answer is yes. And don't change the subject." She began tapping her feet in concert with her fingers. "You and Fran!"

"There is no me and Fran," he said bitterly.

Jo halted her rhythmic tapping and leaned forward in her chair. "Why not?"

"I'm a drunk. Her lousy ex-husband was a drunk. That's it. Finis. End of bad B movie."

"You are not a drunk!" she protested. "You've been in recovery for five years."

"I am now and always will be a drunk. Fran has made a good life for herself. She has two teenagers to finish raising and doesn't need another drunk in her life."

"Fran said that?"

"She doesn't need to. I know it."

"She doesn't know how you feel about her, does she?" Jo asked accusingly.

The phone rang. Ed snatched it up.

"Selkin here," he answered. "Hi, there, yourself," he went on with noticeably greater warmth. "So the deal's on? . . . You mean now, right now? That's terrific! . . . Four minutes? How—oh, right. Car phone. Look, just have the guard phone up. . . . Great. See you."

As soon as Ed hung up, Jo resumed her foot and finger tapping. Who had he been talking to, and what was that about a deal? She was also itching to get the whole story about Fran. But before she could get a word out, he bounced out of his chair and walked over to the door.

"I have the best surprise. Come on." He led the way out the door and down the hall.

"What is it?" she asked, but received no reply.

Chapter Two

Jo tried to catch up with Ed, then slowed when he stopped by the elevator at Linda's desk. Some big surprise—a chat with the most vicious gossip in captivity. Hadn't Ed learned that this particular receptionist thought it was her job not only to answer their calls, but to listen in on them, as well?

Worse yet, Linda had Alex MacHail for company. He smiled at Ed in greeting and slid the smile over to her as she approached. Ed pursed his lips and looked first at Alex, then at Jo, but said nothing.

"Guided tour over already?" Jo asked to fill the silence.

"No," Alex replied. "Ron asked me to meet him here. Apparently something's come up. You know anything about it?"

"Not a thing," Jo replied.

Ed smiled enigmatically.

"You look nice today, Jo," Linda said.

Unusual comment for Linda. She must be up to something. Jo felt rather than saw Alex's scrutiny. So let him look. No movie-star dazzle here, just long brown hair pinned up, brown eyes, regular features and a smidgen of makeup. Her only splash of color was the red silk rose she'd pinned on her lapel to cheer up an ancient navy suit.

"Thanks, Linda, you look nice yourself," Jo replied. How could such a conventional reply be both an understatement and an overstatement? Linda was always impeccably turned out—hair, makeup and clothes invariably up-to-the-minute and flawless. She always looked more than just nice, and she always looked just a little unreal.

"You should see this," Linda said to Jo. She picked up a Hollywood gossip sheet from her desk and handed it across to her, but Alex intercepted it before she could take it.

"It's not all that interesting," he said.

Jo straightened her shoulders. "I'll be the judge of that." She held out her hand. "If you don't mind."

Alex looked over at Linda then back at Jo. He handed her the paper.

"Nick got his picture in *Eye Spy*," Linda said. "That'll be good publicity for the show."

Nick—that explained it. And old Perfect Pecs here had already heard an earful of gossip about her. She snapped the paper and held it up to read it. She'd be darned if she'd let him see it bothered her.

Ed stood next to her and read over her shoulder. The photograph showed a beaming Nick standing on a beach, palm trees visible in the background, his arm around a beautiful woman with an enormous quantity of blond hair, an equally impressive bustline and a bikini so small it was almost nonexistent. The caption revealed the true focus of the photo. "Supermodel Misty Davis, vacationing in the Bahamas with soap hunk Nick Keith. Next month's *Esteem* cover will be her thirteenth for the fashion mag."

Pain, humiliation, anger, desire for revenge—every emotion of betrayal blazed up all over again. Jo tried to make her face a blank mask. She laid the paper down carefully on Linda's desk and bent over it.

"Let's see, what do they have to say about him?" She squinted at the caption. "'*Eye Spy* spots soap punk Nick

Keith in the Bahamas playing Bimbo, Bimbo, Who's Got the Bimbo.'"

"Sorry, Jo. I shouldn't have shown it to you. I can see you're still not over him."

There was a false strain in Linda's voice that made Jo look up quickly. She caught a look both sly and eager, as if she were waiting to feast on Jo's pain. The sheer meanness of it took Jo's breath away, choked off any bright reply, any put-you-in-your-place comeback.

Ed reached over casually and picked up the paper. "Linda, there's an item in here about you," he said. "Did you see it?"

"About me?" Delight fought with disbelief across her face. She stretched her hand out for the paper.

Ed held it just out of her reach. "Let me read it to you. 'There was a young girl from Berlitz, 'Twas accused of being a witch, "Not at all," she denied, and loudly decried, "Everyone knows I'm a—"'"

"That's enough!" Linda's voice was just one shade below screaming. A few curious heads popped out of offices down the hall. She half stood, snatched the paper out of Ed's hand, then plopped back into her chair and stuffed the paper under her desk. Ed watched her with a look of faint amusement on his thin face.

The phone rang, and Linda answered it a bit more curtly than usual. "Countrel Enterprises." Then she said, "One moment please." She looked up at Ed. "It's for you." She slapped the receiver into Ed's outstretched palm.

Ed listened, said, "Thanks," then handed the phone back.

Linda took the receiver with her fingertips, very careful not to touch Ed's hand. "I know you think it's funny to call people names. Perhaps that's what comes from missing your AA meetings."

Ed gazed at Linda for a beat. Then he said softly, "You have informers at my AA meetings? My, that is nasty of you. Just for that, Linda, I'm not going to introduce you to my good friend Madeleine Marne."

"Oh, sure, your good friend," Linda replied with sneering disbelief. And while her face was fixed in that unpleasant expression the elevator doors parted and Madeleine Marne, the legendary movie actress, swept out on a cloud of her own hundred-dollar-an-ounce perfume.

"There you are, Edward," she said chidingly, as if he had been trying to hide from her. She came over and embraced him. A startled Jo noticed that although she only kissed the air in the vicinity of his cheek, she did give him a real hug, which he returned.

"Hello, Madeleine. Nice to see you," Ed replied. He stepped back from their embrace and pointedly turned his back on the now gaping Linda. He put out a hand to Jo and drew her closer. "Madeleine, I'd like you to meet my co-writer, Jo Barnett."

"I'm delighted to meet you, Jo. I've heard so much about you from Edward."

She had? What was going on, anyway? First Linda's mean trick, now Ed's surprise. She shook Madeleine Marne's hand and bobbed her head several times. She couldn't speak, couldn't even manage a simple "Pleased to meet you."

"Don't mind Jo," Ed said. "She's unusually quiet this morning. Enjoy it while it lasts."

Still keeping his back to Linda, Ed put out his other arm in an inclusive gesture. "This is Alex MacHail." Alex stepped toward the little circle. "Alex just joined the show today."

Madeleine shook Alex's hand. "I'm so glad. It's nice not to be the only greenhorn."

Jo stared at them. Wait a minute. What did she mean? Was *the* Madeleine Marne joining "Triumph"? Ed was somehow involved in this casting coup, and he hadn't told her a thing.

Madeleine Marne held Alex's hand for a moment longer than absolutely necessary. She released her grip, dipped her head and looked up flirtatiously through her lashes. Rumor had it that she was partial to younger men. The rumor might just be true. Judging by the goofy smile on Alex's face, it looked as if he had no problem with that at all.

"I believe they're waiting for us in the conference room." Ed offered his arm to Madeleine Marne. "You, too," he said to Jo and Alex. He turned and escorted Madeleine down the hall. Jo and Alex trailed behind.

"Shall I buzz Mr. Fisk?" Linda called after them in a frantic bid for contact.

"No need," Ed said without looking back. "We're expected."

"You have a strangely gleeful look about you this morning, Edward," Madeleine commented.

"Do I? Well, it's because I got even with someone who was being unkind to a friend. And you helped, by the way."

"I did? Oh, good. I think." And she glanced over her shoulder with a raised-eyebrow inquiry at Jo and Alex. Jo smiled and shrugged her shoulders.

Ron stepped out from his corner office, with Bea hovering behind him. They had probably been standing just inside the doorway for some time, waiting for Madeleine Marne's appearance. Jo slowed her pace so she wouldn't have to listen to Ron scrape and fawn. Watching him was a show in itself.

In fact, she didn't even want to see Ron right now. It was bad enough that he had backed out of their agreement to do a mixed-race love story, but to do it in front of Alex Wrong-For-The-Part MacHail was just plain insulting. And here Alex was again, hanging back from the others the same way she was.

"Do you have any idea what's going on? What are we meeting about?" Alex asked quietly. He fixed her with that same intent, just-for-you gaze he'd flashed earlier in the conference room. Why couldn't he leave her alone?

"*We* are not meeting. You will sit down, shut up and smolder, or whatever your specialty is, so Miss Madeleine Marne will think what fun it will be to take this role."

"What role?"

"Exactly."

She went on into the conference room and Alex followed. She waited until he chose a seat, then sat two seats down from him. Ron stood at the head of the table.

"It gives me an incredible pleasure," Ron intoned, "to announce that Miss Madeleine Marne will be joining our show."

Jo shifted in her seat. The urge to doodle suddenly became acute. Why hadn't she brought a notebook?

"I don't have to tell you..." He didn't have to, but he would anyway.

The door opened, and a breathless Fran slipped in and took the empty seat next to Jo. Fran gave Madeleine Marne a startled glance.

"What's going on?" she whispered in Jo's ear.

"Ed knows Madeleine Marne. They're friends, he says. He got her to come on the show," Jo whispered back. "Do you have a pencil and paper with you?"

"A profound honor..." Ron droned on.

Fran produced a pen and a small notebook from her purse and handed them to Jo. Jo flipped open the notebook to a blank page and started making a rapid series of spirals.

"Miss Marne will take the role of Nora Wainwright."

Jo winced. An already-signed role, that would cost plenty in broken contract fees. Jo began to frame the spirals with small triangles.

"Jo, will you give Miss Marne some background on the story line and her role?"

The pen slipped on the last triangle. Jo jerked her head up. "Who, me? It's Larry's story line. I just filled in for Dorothy." Where was Larry, anyway?

Ron gave a hollow laugh. "You know, Miss Marne, this all happened so quickly that we aren't quite all caught up with ourselves and our own staff changes."

Staff changes? What was he talking about? Jo flashed a look at Ed. He gave a little shake of his head. Obviously, he didn't know, either.

"I should probably tell you a little bit about how we do things here at our dream factory."

Jo rolled her eyes. Don't let him start with the tired clichés again. She started filling in the triangles with crosshatching.

"We have two writing teams," Ron went on. "Bea is our head writer. She supervises everything and she writes with the team that does your character. But one member of her team is in the hospital, and the other has just resigned."

Resigned. What a disaster. Jo looked up and saw Ron flash her an I-mean-it look. She had silently, but firmly, been ordered to keep her mouth shut. There wasn't any problem, Miss Marne. We're just short two out of three writers for your story line.

"We expect Dorothy back by the end of the month," Ron said. "And we're going to replace Larry immediately. Meanwhile, we'll shift the writing around a little. Jo, you worked on the Bart Wainwright story line. Can you give Miss Marne some background?"

Jo put the pen down. She took a few seconds to align it perfectly with the side of the notebook. Better make this good, or Miss Madeleine Marne would drop the project as impulsively as she had taken it up.

"Nora Wainwright is the first wife of Bart Wainwright. It hasn't been revealed in the show yet, but Bart has been kidnapped by his cousin, Albert, who has had plastic surgery so he can pass as Bart's double."

"I knew it!" Madeleine Marne exclaimed, leaning forward in her chair. "I knew something wasn't right."

Jo hesitated a moment. Did this mean... "Do you watch the show?"

"Since it first came on the air. Thank God for VCRs. I used to insist we stop shooting so I could watch in my trailer. That caused a certain amount of resentment, I'll tell you. But I just knew something was going on when Bart told Della that he didn't see why they couldn't be good friends. You know he has never forgiven her for not telling him that Stephen was really the baby's father. And another thing, what is he doing going down to the wine cellar all the time?

Bart never gets his own wine. He always has the butler do it.''

Next to Jo, Fran let out a long breath. Jo looked at Ed. He winked at her. She looked at Ron. Ron smiled. And for good reason. Miss Marne watched every day. The characters were like family members. The improbable story lines were accepted without a blink. They could write anything they liked for her. Madeleine Marne was a fan.

"How do you remember all those twists and turns of the plot?'' Alex asked Jo. Everyone was standing at one end of the conference room while commissary staff set the table for a catered lunch. "I got lost when you came to Bart playing Albert playing Bart.''

"I didn't notice you having any trouble when it got around to suggestions for your role as Nora Wainwright's protégé. Especially the part about her wearing down your character's rough edges,'' Jo replied dryly.

"Does that mean I can stop now?'' he asked.

"Stop what?''

"You know—smoldering.'' He gave her a sleepy-eyed smile redolent with sex and desire.

Jo's heart gave a little extra kick, like a small electric shock in her chest. "Yes. You can turn off the smolder.''

He blinked once and changed his expression. Good, he was back to that crinkle-eyed smile. Even so, she'd better watch her step with this one. He was smart—for an actor.

Fran joined them. "Goodness, can you believe it?'' Fran asked them. "She felt the role would be 'more appealing' if there were *several* seductions. And 'it would be amusing' if one of them was with a younger man,'' she said, imitating Madeleine Marne's inflections.

Alex laughed, low and husky, like his speaking voice. "You're a good mimic, Fran.''

Ed, standing with the tight little group around Madeleine Marne, looked over at them. What was he up to, anyway? His famous actress friend hadn't let him leave her side since she'd arrived. Maybe he thought it would make Fran jealous. Maybe he was right.

Ron broke from the herd and headed toward them. Jo steeled herself. "How are you kids doing?" Ron asked, then went on without waiting for an answer. "Way to go, Alex. Madeleine likes you. Jo, thanks for hanging in there after I threw you that curve."

"I'm getting used to your style, Ron," she replied. "You never let your right hand know what your left brain is doing."

"Isn't it never let your—" Ron started to ask, but stopped when the caterer signaled that the lunch was ready to be served. He dashed off to supervise the seating.

Fran gave her a gentle elbow in the ribs. "Jo, please watch it. One of these days Ron's going to figure out that you're making fun of him."

Jo had a comeback ready for Fran, but Alex was standing right there, listening to every word. She settled for making a face.

"You mean she's not supposed to talk to her boss like that?" Alex asked with transparently put-on naiveté.

Fran giggled. "You thought maybe it was in her job description?"

Why was Fran encouraging him? If she'd just ignore him, he'd go away and bother someone else.

"So she's not under contract to produce eight searing verbal put-downs a day?" he asked, eyebrows raised in mockery.

"No," Jo said. "And neither are you." He wasn't going to make her feel guilty about her behavior toward him. So what if she'd been a little rude? She'd had provocation. "I think we're supposed to sit down now."

She moved toward the seat Ron pointed out for her. Fran sat next to her, and Alex took the seat just opposite. Great, she'd have to look at his classic features all through lunch.

"Does anyone know what's gotten into Linda?" Fran asked. "She acted very strangely when I came in. She wouldn't tell me right away where everyone was."

Jo fussed with her linen napkin, smoothing it flat on her lap. Now she'd have to sit through a reprise of the Nick-and-Misty article.

"Linda doesn't like poetry," Alex said.

She looked up at him, surprised. He wasn't going to pass on the juicy parts—at least, not here in public. And he'd tried to keep her from seeing the article, too. Looked as if Ron had hired an actor with a Galahad complex. Or maybe he just wanted to show her up because she'd been so rude.

"It's a bit of a stretch to call Ed's limericks poetry," Jo said.

At the sound of his name Ed looked over at them. "You're challenging my qualifications as a versifier?" he asked with pretended affront.

"Oh, come on," Jo replied. "'A young girl from Berlitz'?"

"I know Berlitz isn't a place," Ed said. "Thought you were criticizing my rhyme scheme. Never got to finish. It ends 'Everyone knows I'm a snitch.' What did you think I was going to say?"

"I know what Linda thought you were going to say," Jo replied.

"No creative imagination. That's why we're writing the scripts and she's answering the phone."

Fran leaned toward Jo. "Linda must have been up to something meaner than usual to provoke Ed that much."

"Yes . . . well." Jo hesitated. She really didn't want to get into it with Fran. First Fran would offer sympathy, then she'd tell her to let go of her anger.

"Jo?" Ron called down from the head of the table. "Alex never got to finish the tour of the studio. How about you hit the high spots with him after lunch?"

What? He couldn't be serious. She clenched her jaw. No writer had ever been asked to play tour guide before, not even to VIPs, which he wasn't. But she couldn't get out of it in front of all these people.

"Sure, Ron," she replied with as little enthusiasm as she dared. Maybe he'd figured out what she'd said to him earlier. She glanced at Alex.

"Thanks," he said to her with a knowing smile. "I appreciate it."

He'd asked Ron to get her to take him around. She just knew it. What nerve.

Jo paused in front of the elevator and turned to Alex. "Shall we take the elevator, or do you prefer the stairs?" she asked. She'd play the part of gracious tour guide to the hilt. Rub his nose in it.

"The elevator, please," he said and pushed the Down button. "It's so much more—private, don't you think?"

What did he mean, private?

The doors opened with a ding and a whoosh. He stood back to let her precede him. She stepped into the elevator reluctantly.

He followed her in, and the doors closed them in. "Don't worry," he said, lounging against the elevator wall. "I just wanted to talk for a minute." He pushed the first-floor button.

"I'm not worried," she lied.

"I sure hope you don't get into too many poker games."

She stuck out her jaw. "And what is that supposed to mean?" Forget the gracious-tour-guide role. She wasn't cut out for it.

"Your face shows everything you're thinking," he replied, a teasing smile showing at the corners of his mouth. "You have a deadpan that's like a neon sign flashing 'I'm joking.' If you could do it on purpose, you'd be a fantastic actor. But you don't even know you're doing it, do you? You say, 'I'm not worried,' but your mouth pulls down at one corner, and your eyes get wide."

He was flirting with her. She couldn't believe it. Clever flirting. And slick, very slick. But why? Hadn't she made it abundantly clear she didn't like handsome, smooth-talking actors?

The elevator bounced to a stop and the doors slid open. Jo straightened her shoulders. "Now that we've had our little talk, why don't I show you around?" She sailed out, chin high.

Alex stayed in the elevator. "That wasn't what I wanted to talk about," he said.

She whirled around. "No? Well, what fascinating topic of conversation were you proposing?"

The elevator doors began to slide shut. Alex pushed the Door Open button and held it down. "I thought you might tell me why it matters if Ed misses an AA meeting."

Of all the nerve. He truly believed she'd gossip with him about one of her closest friends. She put her fists on her hips. "What makes you think I'd tell you anything about that? It's his private business."

"Because I know why he and Madeleine Marne are such good friends," he replied and released the button. The doors slid together.

Jo jabbed at the button in the wall panel, and the doors reopened. She stepped into the elevator. "If you hold the Door Close button, no one can call the elevator," she said.

"Oh, yeah?" He frowned at the panel.

"Here," Jo said, stepping to his side. "This one." She pushed the button and held it down. He hadn't budged when she reached for the button, so they were standing pretty close together. Too close, really. She pressed her lips together and tried to look fierce, tried to let him know she wouldn't put up with any funny business. "Now, how do you know about Ed and Madeleine?" she demanded.

"They told everybody about it," he said. "After lunch. When you were in the ladies' room."

"What?" She dropped her finger from the button and stepped through the elevator doors before they'd even fully opened. This time Alex followed her into the corridor. "Why did you need to tell me in private if everyone already knows?" She strode down the hall. He limped a little more pronouncedly than earlier, but kept up with her. Let him limp. It would serve him right. He'd tricked her.

"I wasn't too sure about the part I asked you about."

"Ed's AA meetings? Everyone knows about that, too. They're a condition in his contract."

"Is that legal?"

"According to Ed, reassurance, not legality, is what counts in this case. He got fired twice before because of his drinking. That was before I knew him." She paused in the doorway to the makeup room. "This is makeup. Next door down is hair." She kept on marching down the corridor. He was going to get the abbreviated tour. "Now tell me how they know one another."

"They went through recovery together, five years ago."

She stopped in her tracks. It was fairly common knowledge that Madeleine Marne had gone into a recovery program. It had never occurred to her that Ed could have been in the same one.

"You didn't know that, did you?" Alex asked. "And I'll tell you something else. He was at the group's annual reunion last Friday night."

What a relief. He really had been at a meeting. He wouldn't lose his job. She didn't think she could face working day after day without Ed—and Fran. Ed and Fran. The two just fit together so well. Why couldn't Ed just tell Fran straight out that he cared about her?

"Is this all there is?" Alex asked.

"What?" She'd let her mind drift. Better get this tour over with. "No. Wardrobe's right down here."

One more turn and they came to the cavernous wardrobe room with its double-tiered racks of clothes and shelf after shelf of Lucite boxes containing every imaginable accessory. Sandy worked in wardrobe, and with any luck she'd be in here now. Sandy had a black belt in flirting. She could take on Alex MacHail, killer blue eyes and all, and not even break a sweat.

"Sandy, are you at home?" Jo called.

"Jo, what are you doing down here?" Sandy's voice came from the back of the room. She emerged from behind a rack of dresses, looking as perfectly turned out as any of the actors she dressed. "You brought company. How nice."

"Sandy, this is Alex MacHail. He's going to play the role of Johnny," Jo said. "Alex, I'd like you to meet Sandy Neale. She'll make sure you're always appropriately dressed."

"Or undressed, as the case may be," Sandy said, widening her eyes in a significant look. "So you're going to be Tracy's new love interest."

"You mean Lorna. That's the role Tracy plays," Jo explained to Alex. Sandy and Tracy had a friendly competition where men were concerned, so Sandy had probably meant to say it that way.

"Do you own a tux?" Sandy asked suddenly.

Alex looked a little taken aback. "Yes, but I got the impression that this character wouldn't wear anything but jeans and a torn T-shirt." He looked at Jo as if for confirmation.

"Not for the show," Sandy said, laying a well-manicured hand on his arm. "For the anniversary party. You'll have to come, you know. Everyone has to. Right, Jo?"

"I'd forgotten all about it," Jo said. "But Sandy's right. It's the fifteenth year for 'Triumph,' so they're giving a big banquet to celebrate. Death is probably the only acceptable no-show excuse. Your own, that is, and then only if rigor mortis has already set in."

"It won't be that bad," Sandy protested. "There'll be dancing. You like to dance, Alex?"

Jo could watch Sandy for hours. She was an artist in her own right, and her performance art project of the moment was to get Alex to go to the banquet with her. He could do worse. Sandy was a lot of fun to be with.

"When is this anniversary party?" Alex asked them.

"Not for a while yet," Jo said. "You have time to train for it."

"Train? You mean for eating? Dancing?"

"No, for listening to interminable, self-congratulatory speeches. Ron's writing his own this year. It'll probably run about ninety minutes."

"Listen up, everyone," someone called from down the hall. "Madeleine Marne is on sound stage one."

Sandy turned wide eyes on Jo. "Did you hear that? Madeleine Marne."

"We know," Jo said. "We just had lunch with her." Sandy had a permanent case of celebrity-itis. She'd pump Jo for hours about that lunch.

"I don't believe this. What are we standing here for? Let's go." She grabbed Alex by the arm and dragged him toward the door.

"She's joining the show, Sandy," Jo called after her. "You'll see her every day."

Sandy didn't pay any attention. Jo followed a little way behind. She should put in an appearance, anyway, show her enthusiasm for the star who'd boost the show into first place for a while. She'd probably see Nick, though, and she couldn't get too excited about that prospect. She trailed behind them down the corridor to the elevator, then made a right turn and was pushed through double doors onto the sound stage by the crowd of people who came up behind her.

What a mob scene. Jo moved along with the crowd, and still got jostled from behind. What in the world made Ron think he could give Madeleine Marne an insider's tour of a working set? Any ordinary group this large was unsettling to the actors and crew. Madeleine Marne's presence was completely disruptive.

Fran and Ed stood in the front row on the other side of the encircled admirers. Sandy and Alex were squeezed in on that side of the circle, too. Sandy gave Jo a warning look and pointed toward the set.

Jo's gaze followed Sandy's pointing finger. Nick, with his perfect square jaw and his perfect blond hair covering his perfectly empty head. He was beckoning to someone off the set to come join him—a woman, of course. What a rotten day of sick surprises. Nick had brought his bimbo to work with him.

She didn't need this. She had to get away, but she couldn't move. A crush of bodies pressed in around her.

"Quiet, everybody!" Ron's voice boomed over the busy hum of voices. "I have some wonderful news. Miss Madeleine Marne will be joining the show in the role of Nora Wainwright."

Applause and cheers burst forth from everyone.

"Now keep it down, will you? I'll make introductions. This is Andy Pierce, our director. And Tracy Randall, who plays Lorna."

Madeleine Marne smiled and nodded.

"This is Nick Keith and . . ." Ron paused, unable to put a name to the next face.

"My girl, Misty Davis," Nick said.

Jo saw a few people turn to look at her. She tried to keep her expression blank.

"Have we met before? You look familiar somehow," Ron said, sounding like a loser at a singles bar. Poor Ron, doomed to unoriginality for life.

"You know, Ditsy Mavis," Ed boomed in a Ron imitation. "Been on the cover of *Esteem* thirteen times."

Misty's toothpaste smile faltered a little bit. A few titters arose from the back rows. Dear Ed. Those who knew him would guess he'd done it on purpose. All eyes were on Ed and Nick.

Jo heard Nick say loudly and emphatically, "It's *Misty Davis*" before she turned and pushed through the crowd. She reached the heavy double doors of the studio. Escape, at last.

"Here, let me get that for you," A voice from behind her said. Alex. He pushed the release bar and held the metal door open for her to pass through.

She gritted her teeth. She really didn't want to have to deal with Alex MacHail anymore. Why couldn't he have stayed behind and succumbed to Sandy's charms?

She stopped in front of the elevator and punched the Up button. Of course, it didn't come. She punched the button again. She'd like to take the stairs, but Alex had planted himself in the middle of the corridor, blocking her path.

"Guess this guy, Nick, has given you a pretty bad time," he said.

What could he possibly know about a bad time? She doubted any woman had ever even broken a date with him, much less broken his heart. Where was that elevator, anyway?

"Are you all right?" he asked.

He probably thought she was going to burst into tears any second. Well, he could hold his breath, because she never cried. At least not anymore. He patted her shoulder tentatively, the way people touched elderly widows at funerals. Did he think she had any use for his condolences? She shrugged him off.

"Look, Galahad," she said. "Unless you're registered with the Bureau of White Knights, don't get any rescue fantasies going. I'm not going to faint, weep, or tear out my hair."

"Does that mean you're okay?"

"Yes. I'm fine," she said through clenched teeth. Someone had probably highjacked the elevator. If he'd only move, she'd walk up the stairs.

"Good. You know, I was wondering about the show's anniversary banquet—since we both have to go, maybe we could go together."

Did he think she wanted his pity? What did it take to get through to him? Okay, he'd asked for it. "I guess I misjudged you. I was under the impression you understood polysyllabic words. Let me make it easy for you. Go away. Leave me alone."

The elevator arrived at last. She marched in, turned around and stared at him. He didn't join her, but he didn't look crushed, either. He looked—interested. She pushed the Door Close button and shut him from her sight.

Chapter Three

"So I follow her into the hallway," Alex said to Lewis, who was hidden from sight behind the industrial-sized refrigerator door. Two of Lewis's employees were busy preparing salads at the other end of the mammoth kitchen. Lewis himself was rummaging around in the refrigerator, but made little "um" noises to let Alex know he was listening.

"She looks upset, which you can figure she would be. I ask her if she's okay. And she gets this uppity look, and says, get this, 'Unless you're registered with the Bureau of White Knights, don't get any rescue fantasies going.'"

Lewis backed away from the refrigerator door carrying a laden tray. He gave the door a nudge with his knee and it closed with a whoosh of cold air. "Were you carrying a hidden tape recorder, or what? How come you keep giving me direct quotes?"

He placed the heavy tray on the stainless steel counter across from where Alex was perched on a stool. With deft movements he selected six bite-sized strawberry tarts and put them on a plate.

"That's what I'm trying to tell you. I remember everything she said. I've never met anyone like her. She's funny and she's smart. She just radiates all this energy. And her face shows everything she's thinking in these little flashes."

Lewis placed the plate of tarts in front of Alex. "Rate these on a scale of one to five. Go clockwise around the plate," he instructed him.

"I'm not sure I'm up to this," Alex protested. "After the pâtés and the seafood quenelles, I'm pretty full."

"Look, Alex, I'm catering for the LaLands tomorrow and they want strawberry tarts. You're my best taster. Help me out."

Alex picked up the first one and popped it into his mouth. "It's good. Fine."

"Go on, eat them all, then say. So what did you do after she said she didn't need your help?"

Alex ate the second one. "I asked her out."

"That's progress. And..."

"And—" Alex paused to eat the third tart "—she told me to go away and leave her alone." He ate the fourth tart.

"Ouch." Lewis wrinkled his forehead in a sympathetic look.

"She's sort of down on men right now. Pretty understandable." He ate the fifth tart. "Actually, I think it's actors she's down on. She seems pretty tight with this guy she works with, the writer."

Lewis gave Alex a long, searching look. "We've known each other a long time," he said.

"Since acting school. What is it, ten years now? You've been a good friend to me." He ate the sixth tart.

Lewis held up his hand. "And you to me. Let's not get into that. What I want to say is, I've never heard you talk like this about anyone before."

Lewis had that right. But he'd never met anyone like Jo before. "I know. I think she's the one."

"What do you mean, you think she's the one?" Lewis objected. "She told you to get lost."

"I can't explain it. Remember, I told you that when I first met Buddy I knew it was meant to be?"

Lewis nodded. "Yeah, I remember."

"Well, that's how I feel about Jo."

"Okay. I'll buy that's how you feel. But these things haven't happened just because you felt it was meant to be. You've made it happen. Look how you worked to get your leg back in shape. Then you found all the right doctors for Buddy. And now you're chasing around with those social workers and the guys in immigration."

"And I'll make it happen with Jo, too."

"I don't know, Alex. It's not the same thing. Sounds like she doesn't even like you."

"She'll like me when she gets to know me better." He checked his watch. "I'd better go. My plane's in two hours. I'll be back Sunday night. I get to spend half the time with Buddy and the other half dealing with red tape."

"How much longer do you think it'll be before you can bring him home?"

"I'm not sure—months, maybe. I can't wait till you meet him." He slipped off the stool. "I gotta go."

"Wait. What about the tarts?"

Alex walked backward across the white tile floor. "The first two were very similar. Good, but not special. The co-conut milk custard tasted weird with the strawberry. The chocolate one was too rich. The lemon custard with the strawberry was fantastic. The best. And the last one was too bland." He reached the door and opened it.

Lewis frowned and nodded. "That tart was a nonfat effort. Guess it showed. Thanks. And Alex?"

Alex paused in the open doorway.

"I can't wait to meet Buddy, and I'd really like to meet Jo, too—when she gets to know you better."

Jo stepped off the elevator onto the third floor. Darn, Linda was already at her desk. She should have taken the stairs. Now she had to pass right by her, and Linda hadn't softened one bit in her attitude toward Jo in the week since the Madeleine Marne incident.

Linda looked up at Jo. "I believe you'll want a copy of this," she said with ice in her voice. She held out a page.

"What is it?" Jo asked. This better not be another article about Nick and his bimbo. Jo took the page and scanned it. It was a memo from Ron banning limerick-writing contests at Countrel Enterprises.

"I don't know what he's talking about," Jo said. She dropped the memo back onto Linda's desk.

"You expect me to believe that?" Linda was fairly spitting. "You and Ed Selkin have been leaving your stupid, insulting poems all over the building. Well, I talked to Mr. Fisk and he's going to put a stop to it."

"I guess you've never heard of the First Amendment. How about I give the American Civil Liberties Union a call?"

Jo turned away without waiting for an answer and headed down the hall to her office. She glanced at her watch. It was only ten in the morning and already a rotten day. First her car had conked out. Then she'd had that exciting tow-truck ride to the garage, followed by a budget-breaking taxi ride to work. And now Linda limericks.

She opened the door to Fran's office without knocking. Fran and Ed were both there.

"What are you doing here?" she snapped at Ed.

"Did my duty and gave Madeleine her seduction scene," he answered, not responding to her peevish tone. "The new writer seems to know his way around a story line, and Dorothy's back today. So Ron sent me back to play on the home team."

"Is something wrong, Jo?" Fran asked.

"My car went down for the count this morning."

"What? The famous Corvair?" Ed teased. "The classic car of the seventies that no one's ever heard of has actually had a—dare I use the word—breakdown?"

"Ed, stop it," Fran said. "You know how attached Jo is to her car. You can see she's upset."

Jo felt herself start to smile. She sank into her usual chair. "You know, Fran, if we could take a core sample of you, the way geologists do of the earth, I bet we'd find nice all the way down."

"What would you find in me, Jo?" Ed asked.

"We would find iron-y," she said. "And I hope we would also find all the possible limericks about Linda you never wrote. Ron put out a memo canceling your contest. Linda is convinced that I am a co-conspirator. I had to threaten to bring in the ACLU."

"Thought you were involved? That's too bad. Guess you were tarred by the same feather," Ed quipped.

Jo put her face in her hands. "Not Addled Adages again. Uncle, uncle."

"What he means to say, Jo," Fran put in, "is that birds of a feather are ridden out of town on a rail together."

Jo lowered her hands. "Not you, too. Aunt, aunt."

"Speaking of rides, I'll give you one after work, if you'd like," Fran said.

"Thanks, but Sandy and I are going to a movie tonight. She'll take me."

There was a tap at the door. "Come in," they chorused.

Alex MacHail opened the door and leaned partway in. It figured. On a day like this one she would have to run into Johnny Handsome.

"Hi." He smiled at her, then at Fran and Ed.

She had to give him credit—he didn't hold a grudge.

"Hey, Alex," Ed said. "How's it going?"

"No complaints, thanks," Alex replied. "I'm here on a mission. Tracy's not happy with some of her lines, so Andy is asking for a script doctor." He looked straight at Jo.

Jo, in turn, looked at Fran. "Pretty please with sugar on top?" she begged.

"Sure, I'll go," Fran said with her usual cheerfulness. She grabbed a pen and notebook. Alex held the door for her and gave Jo an enigmatic look before he closed it behind him.

"He's wondering why you wouldn't go," Ed observed.

"And I'm wondering why Andy sent him instead of phoning up. Maybe he thought Mr. MacHail needed to be taken down a peg or two. Turn him into an errand boy. Give him the proper perspective on working on daytime drama." Jo spun around in her chair.

"Maybe Fran was right. He likes you," Ed said.

Jo gave her chair another spin, then put her feet down hard and stopped abruptly. "And maybe we should leave never-never land now and fly back to the real world. As in you and Fran."

Ed shifted in his chair. "Time to stop yakking. Got a lot of catching up to do."

"Why don't you just ask her out? I know she'd like you to."

"Did she say anything?" His tone was sharp.

"Not exactly," Jo replied. "But your name came up a lot while you were teamed with the new writer. And it seemed to me that she was sort of jealous of Miss Marne."

"Proves nothing."

Jo threw her hands up and let them fall to her lap. "What do you think this is, the National Science Foundation? You don't need proof. Just go for it."

"Been over all that. Won't work."

"Ooh!" Jo reached out as if to grab Ed by the throat. "Sometimes I could just throttle you."

Fran opened the door.

Jo jerked her hands back and folded them decorously in her lap.

Fran came in and sat down. "What's going on?" she asked them.

"Nothing. I was just about to strangle Ed, that's all."

"Don't strangle him yet. The restaurant scene has to be changed pronto. Let's tell Linda to hold all calls, shall we?"

At five o'clock Jo found herself in search of Sandy. She looked for her in wardrobe, but in wardrobe they told Jo to look in makeup. She wasn't in makeup, either. She finally found her in the hairstyling room. Although Jo was drawn there by the sound of Sandy's voice, the first person she saw when she entered the room was Alex MacHail.

He sat, as if enthroned, in the stylist's chair, with Gloria busy spraying something on his hair. Sandy was perched in front of him doing her nails and consulting him about her nail polish. Tracy sat next to him, their newly rewritten script open on her lap.

"This is Peachy Keen and this is Passionate Pink," Sandy said, alternately displaying her left and right index fingers. "Which do you think?" Sandy had mastered many styles of flirting. Jo had seen this one before. Sandy would go up to someone she barely knew and start talking very confidentially, usually inviting an opinion on some part of her wardrobe, hair, or makeup.

"I think this works much better, don't you, Alex?" Tracy asked, pointing to the script.

Instead of answering either questioner, Alex looked into the mirror and said, "Hello" to Jo's reflection. The three women looked over at her.

"Jo, come here and tell me what you think," Gloria requested. She had coated Alex's hair with gel and pulled it back into a ponytail. "We tried different things, but I think this is the best. This gel will look wet even when it's dry. What do you think?"

"I think he looks like a cross between a record producer and a hit man for the mob, but you know it's not up to me," Jo replied.

Tracy and Sandy gave her shocked looks. Well, she wasn't a member of this sultan's harem. She could speak her mind. Alex sat calmly watching her in the mirror, half smiling.

"I think it looks great," Tracy said. "But I hope we can have some scenes with it down. I think long hair on a man is so sexy." She tossed her own luxuriant mane of hair in emphasis.

"Come on, Jo, give me a break," Gloria said. "I know Andy or whoever is directing this segment is the one to okay it. But you can tell me if I'm going in the right direction."

"It's fine, Gloria," Jo answered right away. Alex's blue eyes, even reflected in a mirror, exerted their own pressure. "Don't pay any attention to me, I'm just here to see Sandy."

"What's up, Jo?" Sandy asked, looking up from her carefully enameled thumbnail. She had gone with Passionate Pink without waiting for Alex's decision.

"My car's in the shop and I wondered if you would mind driving me over there to pick it up before we go to the movie."

"Jo, you're going to kill me. I forgot about tonight." She scrunched up her face in a mime of extreme pain. "I'm sorry. I made a date with that set designer I met last month."

"That's okay," Jo reassured her. "Don't worry about it."

"But what about your car?"

"I'll get a ride from someone upstairs. No problem, really." It was a lie, since anybody she would ask had already left. Someday soon she'd have to give it to Sandy straight about canceling out on friends just because a man had asked her out.

"Can we do it next week?" Sandy asked, still looking guilty.

"Sure, next week would be great. Why don't you call me tomorrow?" she said with false heartiness. She waved a general goodbye to everybody and tried to act casual as she walked out the door. She hurried once she was in the hall, and in a minute had reached the door to the stairwell.

"Jo, wait. I want to talk to you," Nick called from behind her.

She stopped and looked over her shoulder. Nick, face set, was striding toward her. "They gave me the new script today," he said, biting out each word.

"So?" This didn't have anything to do with her. Nick's character had been reassigned to the other team.

"I want to know what the hell you think you're doing!"

"I don't know what you're talking about," she said. She turned to leave.

Nick grabbed her roughly by the upper arm and jerked her around to face him. "Oh, sure. You don't know what I'm talking about."

She tried to pull her arm away. What did he think he was doing, grabbing her like this?

"I'm talking about the love scene where I'm supposed to be impotent," he said, his mouth twisted into an unbecoming snarl. "This is a real break for me, playing opposite Madeleine Marne, and you make me look like a fool."

She shouldn't, she mustn't laugh. Not with Nick's face so ugly with anger. She held her breath, but like an irrepressible hiccup, a small giggle came up anyway.

"I'll teach you to laugh at me."

Jo pried at his fingers, but he gripped her arm painfully tight and pushed her back against the wall. Just then Alex materialized behind Nick.

"Hands off, pal," he said.

Nick, his face still distorted with rage, swiveled his head toward Alex. "Get out of here. This is between her and me," he growled.

Alex brought his face within inches of Nick's. "There is nothing between you two. Let go of her. Now." He brought his clenched fist up under Nick's nose. "Or I'll break your face."

Nick dropped Jo's arm and leaped backward with almost comic speed. The second she felt Nick's grip loosen, Jo moved away.

Nick put his hands up, palms out, in front of his face. "Wait a minute. Cool it, fella. See? I let go."

Her arm hurt where Nick had gripped it. What in the world had gotten into him?

Alex put his arm around her waist and pulled her gently to his side, placing his body in the way of Nick's path. With a brief look backward at the still-cowering Nick, she let Alex guide her down the hall.

They said nothing to one another as they took turns signing out at the front desk. But as soon as they reached the

front door and Jo figured they were out of earshot of th
guard, she said, "I didn't really need..."

Alex placed two fingers across her lips. "Hush. It's a
right. I'm registered now."

She pushed his hand away. "You're what?"

"Registered. With the Bureau of White Knights. I got m
learner's permit," he said with complete seriousness.

Jo leaned her head sideways until it rested against th
glass of the door. Her eyes ached as if she were about t
burst into tears, of all the ridiculous things. "You were ju
about to punch somebody's lights out, and now you mak
jokes?"

"I just threatened to punch his lights out. And you mad
the joke first," he reminded her.

She lifted her head up with a snap. "You mean yo
wouldn't have hit him?"

He gave a little shrug. "I don't know. I didn't need t
Just the idea of a broken nose and a ruined profile was a
it took," he answered with a grin. He pushed the door open
"Let's go."

She began to back away. "Look, I was going to take
taxi, anyway...."

"Why do you think I was right there when that jerk ha
you cornered?"

"I don't know. Why?"

"I was coming after you to offer you a ride."

"Oh."

"So will you come on?" He gestured toward the door h
still held open. She nodded and stepped through the door
way.

He led her across the parking lot to a gray four-door se
dan. He unlocked the passenger door and held it open fo
her. Jo looked at the car, then looked back at Alex.

"This is your car?" Now, why had she said that? But th
words were out of her mouth and she couldn't take then
back.

He gave her a level look. "What's wrong with it?"

"There's nothing wrong with it. It just doesn't seem like the kind of car you'd drive," she mumbled.

"You know absolutely nothing about me." His tone was neutral, but his mouth was set in a firm line. "Will you get in the car?"

She got in and waited while Alex walked around to the driver's side. She watched out of the corner of her eye as he lowered himself somewhat stiffly into his seat, then switched on the engine and backed out of the parking space. Jo crossed her arms in what she hoped was a casual gesture and felt for the sore place on her left arm. A stab of pain made her pull her hand away with a small jerk. Her arm was too tender to touch.

Alex turned briefly to look at her. "Are you all right? Did he hurt you?" he asked.

All of a sudden the ache in her eyes turned to water. Dammit, why did he have to fuss over her? She turned her head and looked out the side window. Alex had exited the parking lot and was driving down the street. "I'm fine." Her voice wobbled. She felt two tears course down her cheeks.

He pulled the car over to the curb and switched off the motor. "You're crying," he stated.

"I'm not crying. I never cry." Her voice didn't wobble this time, but she felt a third tear follow the wet track down her cheek.

"Oh, God. You're crying and I don't have a clean handkerchief." He sounded nearly desperate. Jo turned her head to look at him. He was patting his pockets with frantic gestures. "I don't even have a dirty handkerchief."

The tears stopped welling up in her eyes. "Are you nuts, or what?"

He wrapped his arms around the steering wheel and rested his head on them. "They'll revoke my learner's permit," he said in a muffled voice.

She gave a begrudging laugh then. She couldn't help herself. Alex lifted his head and grinned at her.

"I know what. You could use my sleeve." He offered h
nearest arm to her.

"No, thanks. I'll use my own." She swiped at her cheel
with her coat sleeve.

He switched on the engine again. "Okay. How abou
some directions?"

"Take the San Diego freeway, then exit at Thornton. It
not too far."

Alex followed her directions and soon they were in th
thick of the commuter rush hour.

"What kind of car did you think?" Alex asked.

Had she missed some part of the conversation? "What?

"You said this didn't look like the kind of car I'd drive
What kind of car did you expect?"

"Um, well, let me see. An import. German. A Porsche o
a BMW. Probably a Porsche." She pointed to the righ
"That's the exit up there."

He eased the car over into the exit lane. "Do you just d
the make, or do you do the whole thing? Like what color?

"Black."

"Year?"

"I don't know. That depends on how much money you'v
been making. But not the newest model."

Alex drove the car down the exit ramp and halted at th
red stoplight.

"Turn left here," she directed. "It's just after the thir
light on the right."

"Do you do this with everyone? Guess their car?"

"I used to. Car-ma was one of our first games. You know
Fran and Ed and I. We make up games."

"So I noticed. Why?"

"Why? Because otherwise you take it all too seriously an
become like Bea, who's a wonderful writer but she's goin
to smoke herself to death. We'd rather laugh. We made u
a whole chart of personality types by car, like astrologica
signs. Ron was a Mercedes with Jaguar rising. A month late
he traded in his Mercedes for a Jaguar. We laughed all day.

"What's your automotive sign?" he asked.

"Guess," she said, giving him a sideways glance.

"You're going to let the new kid play?" He echoed her aunt.

Jo winced inwardly. She had said a number of not too nice things to him that first day. He hadn't seemed to mind, but then, he was an actor.

"Sure. Why not?" she replied.

"Is there some trick to this? Some rule you haven't told me about?"

"There's no trick, except that you'll never guess." She tried not to sound smug.

"Do I get any clues?"

"Yes. You can have three clues. First clue." She held up her index finger. "I really love cars."

"You really love cars." He paused, seeming to mull over his answer. "Then my guess is that it's a classic car. I might guess an old Jaguar roadster, like the 125 XKE, but I don't think so. How about another clue?"

"All right," she said and gave him a little smile. "Clue number two. It's not a foreign car."

"Hmm. An American classic. I might guess the Ford Thunderbird, circa 1960. But that still doesn't sound right to me."

"Your third and last clue. You're a decade off."

"I'm getting warm, then. Let's see," he said slowly. "An American car, 1970s model. A classic, therefore no longer in production. It could only be a Corvair. Am I right?"

How did he guess? No one ever guessed her car. Many people didn't even know what a Corvair was. Jo turned her head slowly toward him. "I don't believe it."

"I was right? What's the matter, am I supposed to guess the color, too? Let me see." He pursed his lips and knitted his brow. It was too exaggerated. Something was slightly off.

"Red. It has to be red," he pronounced. They pulled up in front of the garage. He switched off the engine and shifted in his seat to face her.

"You already knew, didn't you?" She couldn't keep the irritation out of her voice. "Let me take a wild stab. Sandy

and Tracy had a captive audience, am I right? My guess i
you got all the hot gossip and then some.''

"They didn't tell me you were a sore loser. Remember
asked you for the ground rules.''

"I'm not a sore loser. You cheated," she accused.

He leaned forward slightly. "I didn't cheat. Why are yo
so grouchy? You're the one who said you'd rather pla
games and laugh.''

Jo jerked her head around to look out the side window
She jabbed at the electric window switch several times. Ale
turned the ignition key. She jabbed one last time, and th
window hummed down. What a rotten day and here she wa
taking it all out on Alex. "Psychologists call it displace
ment," she said, still not looking at him. "Nick is a creep t
me, so I am awful to you. Then you go home and kick th
cat.''

"Now, there's something they didn't tell me. That yo
read psychology books.''

"No. I got that in Psychology 101. I don't suppose yo
took psychology courses in college.''

"No, I took evasive action.''

She turned to look at him. "What?''

"It's what you take when your father wants you to go int
his business and you want to be an actor. I'll tell you abou
it some time. Right now, don't you think you'd better ge
your car?''

"Oh. Right." Jo put her hand on the door latch. "Thank
for the ride and for, um, everything.'' Couldn't she come u
with anything better than that?

Alex started to get out on his side of the car. "You ca
just drop me off here. I'll be fine,'' she protested.

"I'd like to see your car, if that's all right with you. I lik
cars, too.''

"Sure, that's fine. I have to talk to Hector." She indi
cated the direction to find her car, then walked into the smal
office adjacent to the work bays where one car was still u
on the hydraulic lift.

"Hey, Hector," she said to the man in mechanic's overalls standing at the counter. "How's my car?"

Hector gave her a mournful look. "I called you twice," he said. "I left messages. I can't get the parts till the day after tomorrow."

Jo brought her fist down on the counter with a thump. "Ooh, that expletive-deleted Linda."

Hector's expression switched rapidly from sorrow to fright. "I'm sorry, really I am. But you can't just pick up these parts—"

"I'm not mad at you, Hector." Jo broke in to reassure him. "It's someone at work. When she gets *really* mad at me, I don't get my messages."

Alex stepped through the office door. "What's the problem?" he asked.

"My car isn't ready. Hector can't get the part until the day after tomorrow." She turned to Hector. "Today's Thursday, so that means, don't tell me, Monday?"

Hector switched on the mournful look again. "I'm afraid so."

"What an unbelievable hassle." Jo rubbed her forehead wearily. "Look, I'm sorry to have dragged you all the way down here for nothing," she said to Alex.

"That's okay. Come on, I'll drive you home." He turned toward the doorway.

"Please don't bother," Jo protested. "I'm sure it's completely out of your way."

Alex turned back to face her. "Oh, yeah? Where do you live?"

"Well, it's sort of east L.A.," she hedged.

"You still live in that apartment building they're trying to tear down?" Hector asked.

Jo nodded in reply.

Hector gave her another of his mournful looks. "I don't know how you take it. One day no lights, one day no water."

"They had to stop that. Our tenants' association got a lawyer and he made them turn everything back on."

"This is sounding more and more intriguing," Alex said. "Let me take you home, and on the way you can tell me about your tenants' association."

Jo walked with Alex back to his car. She probably shouldn't go along with this, but he had a way of making it hard to refuse.

Alex exited the freeway where Jo indicated. "Let me see if I've got this straight," he said. "You still pay rent, but you pay it into a special bank account?"

Jo nodded. "That's right. That way we show our good faith to Cranshaw Construction. We'll pay our rent, we just won't pay it to them until they meet their obligations to us. Turn left at the next light."

"Their obligation being to find you all comparable housing."

"Exactly. This redevelopment business is just a big scam. They're going to tear down a perfectly good building with low rents. And put up a not so good but newer building with higher rents. Turn right at the next corner."

Jo shifted around in her seat. Alex had been kind enough to drive her all over town. Now she had to find a nice way to thank him without prolonging things. She looked down at her hands and started tracing invisible doodles on her lap with her finger. That horrible scene with Nick kept replaying in her mind. What was his problem, anyway? Time to find a quiet corner and lick her wounds. She clenched her hands into fists. Oh, forget Nick. What was she going to do this weekend without a car?

"I thought you said you lived in a quiet neighborhood," Alex commented.

Startled, Jo looked up. A crowd of people was milling around on the sidewalk in front of her building. And a police car sat in the middle of the street, emergency lights flashing.

Chapter Four

"What in the world?" Jo unsnapped her seat belt and grabbed the door latch. She waited until Alex pulled the car to the curb, then swung the door open and jumped out. She quickly scanned the crowd. Most of the people were from the neighborhood or her building. There were a couple of uniformed men, too. They weren't police, because their uniforms were tan, though they seemed to be trying to get the crowd to disperse. Nobody budged.

The familiar face of her tenants' association lawyer emerged from the crowd. He spotted her and began to make his way toward her. Something bad must have happened.

"What's going on?" Alex said right at her elbow.

"That's what I'm about to find out." She sounded calmer than she felt.

Mr. Gomez squeezed between two onlookers and joined Jo and Alex on the outer fringes of the crowd.

"I have some bad news," he said.

"We lost our case, didn't we?" she asked, knowing the answer before he even said a word.

"The judge denied our appeal to stay the evictions. The sheriff's department is delivering them now. Everyone has seventy-two hours to move out. I'm so sorry."

Jo reached out to clasp his hand. "Don't be sorry, Mr. Gomez. I know you tried your best."

The lawyer gave her a sad smile. Jo squeezed his hand before she released it. Between Hector and Mr. Gomez, too many mournful looks had come her way today. There should be a legal daily limit.

"There is some good news, too," Mr. Gomez said. "The judge will hold a separate hearing on whether you have to pay Cranshaw the back rent. We may be able to keep that money for you, because Cranshaw never fulfilled their stipulated requirement of finding housing for all the tenants."

Jo took a step backward and bumped up against Alex's hard chest. She tried to move away and stumbled. He clasped her upper arms and steadied her, but the pressure on her sore arm made her jerk away.

"Sorry," said Alex. He released his grip and stepped around to her side. "That arm's pretty bruised, isn't it?"

"It's a little tender, that's all." She squared her shoulders. "So, where do I pick up my notice?" she asked Mr. Gomez.

"The shorter deputy over there has them." He pointed to one of the uniformed men.

Jo marched over and announced, "I believe you have an eviction notice for me. Name's Jo Barnett."

The deputy thumbed through a batch of manila envelopes. "Josephine Alice Barnett? Apartment 3C?"

Jo gave a sharp nod of her head. The deputy handed her a clipboard and asked her to sign her full name. He pointed to the signature line with a stubby finger then held out a pen. She signed and took her envelope.

"Josephine Alice?" an amused voice asked from behind her.

She swung around to face Alex. "Want to make something of it? I'm sure your original name was just as bad.

Probably something along the lines of Albert McBugg the Third, right?"

"I wasn't making fun. Honest," Alex protested. "The name suits you. It's perfect."

"Same to you, McBugg." She looked down at the envelope she held in her hand. Seventy-two hours to find a new place to live, and she didn't even have a car. Is this how people ended up sleeping on the street with all their worldly possessions in rusty grocery carts?

"Look, Alex, it's been an awful day. I'm tired and—"

"Hungry," he filled in. "Me, too. Any good restaurants around here?"

Jo closed her eyes and let her head sink wearily to her chest. Food. Not really what she had in mind, but it suddenly seemed like a good idea. There was nothing much to eat in her soon-to-be former apartment, anyway.

Her neck was stiff. She rolled her head to the side and then rolled it farther until it was hanging back. She opened her eyes to find that the fading sun had painted the sky in iridescent pastels of pink and orange. Well, now, it wasn't a completely rotten day after all. Here was all this beauty just waiting to be noticed. She brought her head upright and straightened her shoulders.

"There's a Mexican restaurant about three blocks from here. Mind if we walk?" she asked. "And there'll be no more white-knighting it. We'll split the bill."

A waitress seated them right away at a small wooden table. The warm air inside the restaurant was thick with the smell of cooking. One sniff and Jo's stomach started growling.

"Mind if I ask a personal question?" Alex asked from behind his menu.

Jo left hers flat on the table and folded her hands on top of it. "Probably," she answered.

He lowered the menu and looked at her. "Why do you live in this neighborhood when you make enough to live someplace five times more expensive?"

Jo leaned back in her chair and crossed her arms. "You mean my dear friend Sandy, and your leading lady, Tracy, didn't tell you everything about me?"

"I think I left just about the time they were getting to the really good stuff."

Jo gave a disgusted snort. "Okay, I'll tell you. Then let's please drop the subject."

Alex gave a brief nod of agreement.

"I'm the sole support of my widowed mother and younger sister."

Alex looked at her for a long moment. He blinked slowly, once. His eyebrows came together in a little frown. "When did your father die?"

"When I was nine," she replied.

Alex gave her a startled look.

"No," Jo went on, "I haven't supported them since I was nine. Here's the story, and it's better than any daytime drama I could have written. My father died, and my sister was born in the same week. My mother ruined her health trying to support me and my sister, and now I support them." And that was all she intended to say on that topic. She looked pointedly at his menu. "Have you decided what to order?"

He raised his menu again, then peered over the top of it at her. "What do you recommend?" he asked.

"I always have the same thing. *Número dos.*"

He glanced down at the menu, then back at her. She couldn't see his mouth, but his eyes were crinkled at the corners. "Hmm. Always chicken enchilada, rice and beans. No adventuring into the land of *enchilada verde,* or *pollo con mole?*"

Jo knew teasing when she heard it, but didn't rise to the bait. A pretty young waitress with Maria on her name tag came and stood by their table, order pad at the ready and pencil poised.

"Are you ready to order?" she asked, her eyes fastened on Alex. He looked up and smiled at her, and she dimpled back at him.

"Sí," he replied. *"La señorita quiera número dos, y yo quiero... número dos. Dos números dos, por favor."*

The waitress made a hasty scribble on her pad, then bent to pick up Jo's menu from the table. Alex handed over his.

"I wonder if you would do me a favor," Alex said to the waitress, giving her the full blast of his blue eyes. The waitress turned on the dimples again and tipped her head to the side. "Could you please bring us some crushed ice and another napkin?"

The waitress smiled and nodded her head rapidly several times, eagerness to please in every nod and every flash of her dimples. Jo leaned far back in her chair and pulled her crossed arms tighter across her chest. How many times had she had to sit through this kind of byplay with Nick? *Of course the waitress will bring the ice for you, Mr. McHunk. She'll walk all the way to Alaska if she has to.*

The woman bustled off, and Alex turned to look at Jo. She glared back at him. "Something wrong?" he asked.

"I can order for myself, thank you very much," she said through clenched teeth. "I do not suddenly take on a cloak of invisibility just because you're talking to an attractive female."

He gave her a blank look. "Cloak of invisibility? I don't know what you're talking about."

"Of course you don't. It's just second nature to charm every woman you come in contact with."

Alex crossed his arms across his chest, mirroring Jo. "It can't be second nature. You obviously aren't charmed."

She gave him an angry stare. "You got that right."

He stared right back. The waitress hurried up to their table carrying a glass of crushed ice and a cloth napkin on a tray. She quickly unloaded the tray and left.

"So, you have a big ice-eating habit? It's the sign of a vitamin deficiency, you know," Jo sniped at him.

Alex looked down at the glass in front of him for a moment. Then he uncrossed his arms and leaned forward. "The ice is for your arm," he said, his voice quiet and self-contained.

"My arm?" Jo asked.

"For pain and bruising. You're supposed to put it on right away, but you were busy being evicted." He gave her a little smile, which she didn't return.

He unfolded the napkin and tipped some of the ice onto it. "I just thought that if we wrapped some of this in a napkin, we could tie it around your arm while we eat."

"Get something straight, McBugg," she said in a louder voice. "I didn't need you to rescue me from Nick." Out of the corner of her eye, she saw other diners turn their heads. "And I don't need your first aid," she said more softly.

"The name is MacHail." He emphasized each word. "And I didn't notice you stopping him from manhandling you."

"I can take care of myself." She clenched her jaw so tightly she almost ground her teeth.

Just then the waitress brought their dinners to the table. Jo stared down at her steaming plate. How did she get herself into this? She shouldn't have accepted a ride from Alex in the first place.

"Jo," Alex said finally. "Would you listen to me? I think you have me mixed up with somebody else."

Jo picked up her fork and poked at the food on her plate. She had gone off the deep end again for no reason. It was getting embarrassing. What did she care if Alex flirted with waitresses?

"Honest," he said. "You could never be inaudible—I mean invisible."

Jo kept her head down and hid her smile. She had to give him credit, he was funny. She secured a bite of enchilada on her fork, and slowly lifted her head. It was time for a truce, at least until they'd eaten dinner.

She offered a conversational white flag. "So where did you learn to speak Spanish?"

He didn't answer right away. "I broke my leg while shooting on location in Mexico," he finally said. "I ended up in a hospital in Mexico City, and I picked up some

Spanish there. It's a nice language. I'm trying to learn more."

"Were you in the hospital a long time?"

"Mmm," he replied.

Jo ducked her head and took a bite of food. Okay, so his hospital stay was a dead end topic of conversation. She'd just have to go for the old get-him-to-talk-about-himself routine.

"What did you mean when you said you took evasive action instead of going to college?" she asked.

He lounged back in his chair and gave her a lopsided grin. "I had a feeling you'd remember that."

He really did have a charming way about him. It went well with his knockout good looks. Not that she had any interest in him herself. Nick had put an end to her romantic fantasies.

"So tell," she prompted.

"My dad wanted me to go into his business, but I wanted to be an actor. It's an old story. You've probably written that one for the show yourself."

She put her fork down. He wasn't going to get her off the scent of this story. "You still haven't told me what you did."

"I invested most of the money he gave me for my first year's tuition, got a job as a waiter and took acting classes instead."

She leaned slightly forward. "You invested it? In what?"

"Stocks. My dad gave me my own portfolio when I was thirteen. Taught me all about the market. I was pretty good at it, too, which was a big mistake. If I'd been hopeless, he might've eased up on the pressure."

"Wouldn't it have been easier just to tell him how you felt?"

He picked up his water glass and gazed into it. "I tried. He wouldn't listen. Until he didn't get my first semester grades. Then he came around—after a while." He took a sip of water. "Of course, it helped that my investments did well," he added.

"Couldn't you have taken acting classes at the university?"

He frowned slightly. "It's not the same thing. Those are just kids playacting. They're not serious adults working at their craft."

"Single-minded, aren't we?"

He leaned back in his chair and sighed. "I used to be. I centered my whole life around my career. But now I know there are other things in life."

Jo waited for him to go on, but he didn't elaborate. She let the topic drop and devoted herself to her food. Alex seemed to be equally comfortable talking or being quiet. That was a pleasant surprise, but then, he'd been a bit of a surprise all the way down the line. She looked over at him. He really was a pretty nice guy. He'd called it right—she'd mixed him up with Nick.

Alex glanced up at her. "Why are you looking at me like that? Do I have salsa all over my face, or something?" He dabbed at his chin with a napkin.

Jo blinked rapidly. "No salsa. You're fine. I was just thinking, you're—well, you're nice."

He raised his eyebrows. "That's it. I'm nice?" He shifted in his seat. "What about all that other stuff you said about me when you first met me? You change your mind?"

What was he talking about? "What stuff?"

"You remember—Michelangelo jaw, sexy lips, impressive pecs."

"Didn't get your minimum daily requirement of compliments today—is that it?"

"The way you said it wasn't a compliment. You sounded like I should go out and get plastic surgery."

That hadn't occurred to her. She peered at him. "Have you?"

"No. Any other personal questions? Feel free to ask," he said with a wave of his hand.

Jo bit her lip.

"Come on," he said cajolingly. "Don't you want to know my vital statistics—age, weight, marital status?"

"What's it to me?" How had the conversation slipped onto this track?

"I know yours, for one thing. Only seems fair. I'm twenty-eight and never married."

"You skipped weight."

He pushed his chair slightly away from the table. "After this meal, it's twenty pounds more than it was. You want anything else—coffee?"

"No, thanks. I'd better be getting home now. I need to figure out what I'm going to do." She took her napkin from her lap and placed it on the table.

Alex signaled to the waitress for the check, then turned back to Jo. "It's going to be hard to look for a new place without a car."

"You're telling me. I guess I could rent one."

"Look, I've got this great shooting schedule, and I don't have to work tomorrow. I'll drive you around, if you'd like."

"Why would you want to spend your day off doing that?"

"You just said it—because I'm a nice guy."

"Look, I want to get something straight. I'm not interested in . . . in . . ." How could she put this delicately?

"Yes?"

"You know, fooling around."

"No problem. How about hanky-panky?"

She stared at him.

"No?" he went on. "Then what do you say to footsies?"

She let silence fall between them, then said, "Are you done making fun of me?"

"I only asked if you'd like me to drive you around to look at apartments. That's all."

Sounded reasonable, said like that, but something about him made her feel edgy. Probably safer just to rent a car. "It's really nice of you to offer. . . ."

"Fine. How does eleven sound to you?"

Before Jo could answer, the waitress came up to their table and put the check down next to Alex.

"Here's our check," he said, picking it up. "Let's see, do you want to do the math, or shall I?"

Alex carried his ungainly load of empty cardboard boxes into the middle of Jo's studio apartment. It was nicer in here than he'd expected from the outside. Small, but with fresh white walls and furniture in bright colors.

He lowered the cartons halfway to the floor. His knee gave a twinge of protest. Damn leg. It was so much better, he kept forgetting what he couldn't do—like deep knee bends. He let the boxes fall with a thud and turned to Jo, who was practically invisible behind her own load of boxes.

"Here, let me help you with those," he said. He took the boxes from her and dropped them with a thump next to the others.

She looked down at the boxes, then back up at him. "Thanks, but I could have dropped them just as well myself, Galahad. You know, we do have to think about the neighbors below."

"Sorry," he said. She was all grumpy again. Maybe he was pushing it a bit. But his idea of stopping to get packing boxes had seemed the perfect way to get invited up to her apartment.

She shoved one pile of boxes into an empty corner of the room. "Forget it. I should thank you for saving me a lot of time by picking these up tonight. I—" She stopped talking abruptly and gazed at him for a moment.

"What now?" He put his hands on his hips. She'd kept him on his toes all evening—stubbornly independent one minute and suspicious of his motives the next.

"It's your leg," she said softly, almost like talking to herself. "You can't bend your leg all the way. I noticed that when you got in the car."

He shoved his hands into his pockets. She wanted to talk about his leg—his least favorite topic of conversation. "Very observant, Sherlock."

She crossed to her desk and grabbed a pen and pad of paper. "That's a perfect bit for Johnny," she said while she wrote. "Hang on to that piece of business." She looked over at him. "You know, the hands into the pants pockets. Hunch the shoulders."

He clenched his jaw. "I don't hunch."

She pointed her index finger at him. "That's good, too. Just like that." She stared at the pad in front of her, her left hand moving as if playing arpeggios on a piano. "This'll be a great scene." She jotted rapid notes. "In the restaurant. You're busing tables. Lorna's there, of course. Lots of looking, then looking away. Air thick with sexual tension."

Alex pulled his hands out of his pockets and went over to the one easy chair in the room. What next? If he tried to make a pass at her, she'd probably write that in, too. He lowered himself into the chair. She'd probably written more seductions than he'd actually pulled off.

"We'll do the whole bit," she said while still writing. "You'll drop something rather than set it down. And Lorna will realize why and try to help you. You'll get defensive and push her away."

"I know you've had to rework the script for me. I appreciate it." He'd appreciate it more if she'd let down her guard with him.

She stopped writing and looked over at him. "Just mention my name with gratitude in your Emmy acceptance speech," she said, brown eyes sparkling.

His Emmy acceptance speech—how had she known he'd already fantasized about it? He shifted his gaze away from hers. She'd think he was the biggest egomaniac in Hollywood if she knew he'd already planned his speech. Or maybe not, if she knew he wanted to win it for Buddy. He turned his gaze back to Jo. What would she say if he told her?

"Don't look at me like that," she said. "It could happen. I haven't seen your work yet myself, but everyone else is impressed. And these folks don't impress easily."

"Why don't you go win your own Emmy?" he asked, like a kid throwing a dare.

"Maybe I will. Maybe we'll both win. Wouldn't that be something?" she said with a smile.

No, you're something. He held her gaze for a long moment. Her smile faltered, and for an instant her eyes darkened, her lips parted slightly and a trace of pink tinged her cheeks. Then she turned abruptly back to her desk, snatched up her pen and scribbled something on her notepad.

Alex leaned his head against the chair back. Let her turn away. He had what he'd been waiting for since he'd first met her—that flash of awareness. She'd felt the attraction between them, no question about it.

She put down her pen and turned toward him. "Thanks for thinking of the boxes. If you don't mind, though, it's late, and . . ." She let the sentence trail off.

He was on his feet in an instant and heading for the door. "Glad I could help," he said. No point in trying to push things too quickly tonight. He could wait—until tomorrow.

She followed him slowly to the door, keeping a wide distance between them. Did she think he was going to make a grab for her?

He opened the door. "Good night, Jo," he said over his shoulder. "See you tomorrow."

"About apartment hunting tomorrow," she said. "I don't think—"

"I'm all set for eleven," he interrupted her. If he let her get out of tomorrow, they'd be back to square one. "See you then."

He closed her door and hurried as fast as his leg allowed down the three flights of worn stairs. That eviction couldn't have been better timed. She shouldn't be living here. Her apartment was nice enough for what it was, but the neighborhood left a lot to be desired.

He pushed open the scarred front door, passed into the night air and headed for his car. Timing was everything. She needed a nice place to live, and it so happened he had a very nice house. He smiled to himself. Yeah, his house would be perfect for her.

He got in his car, lowering himself into his seat more carefully than he had earlier. Good thing she hadn't seen this maneuver. She'd have written a whole week's worth of scripts around it. Or made a joke. Or done something he couldn't even guess at ahead of time.

He started the car and retraced his earlier route back to the freeway. Jo living in his house—it was the perfect solution. They could find out if they were right for each other. And, if she liked kids, then maybe Buddy would have a *mama* and a *papi*. Boy, Buddy would love that. Every time he went down there for a visit Buddy asked if he'd found a *mama* yet, because he wanted *una familia grande*. And he'd stretch his little arms out as wide as they'd go.

Look at me, imagining marrying her, and I haven't even kissed her yet. He would, though, and soon. Some things were just meant to be—he knew that now. All he had to do was convince Jo to move in. The rest would take care of itself.

Chapter Five

As always, Jo woke up like a deep-sea diver surfacing from murky depths. Today she came up too fast, and got a bad case of the bends. How else could she have ended up standing in the middle of the room before she actually came awake?

She staggered back to her bed and sat down. She was in her apartment, wasn't she? Yes. Piano, desk, computer, modem, fax that side. Kitchen alcove over there. She closed her eyes and fell sideways onto her pillow. Something was not quite right, though—all those boxes. She opened her eyes. Now she remembered. She had to move out. The question was, where would she go? She pulled the pillow over her head. She couldn't think with that awful pounding noise.

"Jo, open up."

She lifted the pillow. Nick? What was he doing here?

"Jo, open the door."

"Go away, Nick," she yelled without moving from her half-prone position on the bed.

"Please, Jo. I have to talk to you." He started pounding again.

She slung the pillow to the other end of the bed and pushed herself upright. "I am going to kill you, Nicholas Keith," she muttered.

She heaved herself off the bed and made her way to the door. Her fingers fumbled with the lock. She cracked the door. There stood Nick behind an armful of long-stemmed red roses.

"Hi, Jo." He gave her one of his famous boyish smiles.

She scowled back. "How did you get in the building?"

"The front door was open. Some people are moving out. Can I come in?" He edged forward.

Jo stepped back and opened the door to let him in. Then she closed it and leaned her back against it.

"These are for you." He held out the roses to her.

She made no move to take them. "What do you want, Nick?"

He walked over to the kitchen alcove, propped the flowers stem down in the sink and turned back to face her. "I want to apologize for my behavior yesterday. I'm very sorry. There was no excuse for it."

"You got that right." She ran her fingers through her tangled hair to comb it back from her face.

"I'm sorry I woke you up. You were always such an early riser, I thought you weren't opening the door on purpose."

She watched him taking in her messed-up hair and cotton knit nightshirt. "That's right, Nick. Still the same old frumpy me. Your black lace contribution to my glamorous new self is over there." She pointed to a pile of folded clothes. "My gift to the Salvation Army."

He looked around the room at the piles of books and cardboard boxes. "What's going on?"

"I'm moving, and so are you." She reached behind her and grabbed the doorknob.

He gave her a surprised look. "I won't stay. But I was hoping you'd at least accept my apology." He put on a very sincere expression. "I really feel terrible about the whole thing."

"I won't file charges for assault and battery. That's as good as you'll get out of me." She turned the handle and pulled the door open. "Now make like a man on a leaky boat and bail."

His surface of sincerity gave way to a petulant frown. He shouldered his way past her. Jo slammed the door behind him.

"I really feel terrible about the whole thing," she mimed in a high voice. She stomped over to her upright piano. "What a phony!"

She plopped onto the piano bench and reached blindly for some music on top of the piano. "'Great Symphonies Transcribed for the Piano'," she read aloud. "That should do just fine." She slammed into the first movement of Beethoven's Fourth Symphony. She saw the notations to shift to pianissimo and mezzo piano, but she ignored them and played every chord a satisfying fortissimo. Forget the fine points and subtle contrasts of loud and soft, this was music therapy.

The music took over, as it always did, and everything slipped away except the sounds that she created and bathed herself in. Loud pounding on the door stopped her midphrase. She jumped up from the piano bench.

"Nick, you're going to make the cover of *Time* as jerk of the year."

She strode to the door and threw it wide open. "Okay, you asked for—" Alex stood in the doorway. She closed her mouth with a snap and blinked furiously at him. "What are you doing here?"

"We did say eleven, didn't we? What's going on?" He looked over her shoulder into the room behind her.

"Nothing's going on. I thought you were Nick."

"Nick?" he echoed, his face set with disapproval.

She didn't need this. Why hadn't she canceled out on him last night? For that matter, why had she let him talk her into his helping her in the first place?

"May I come in?" he asked, stepping into the room and closing the door behind him.

She took several steps backward. "Look, I'm not even dressed yet."

"So I see," he said, letting his gaze trail slowly from her face, over her brief nightshirt to her bare toes.

He didn't touch her, but traces of heat, like warm fingers, followed the path of his gaze nevertheless. She folded her arms across her breasts, hands clasping her upper arms, and then winced at the tender soreness of her left arm. She glanced down and saw the green-and-purple bruising through her spread fingers. She looked up at Alex, who was watching her.

He shoved his hands deep into his pockets. "Did he kiss it and make it better?"

She spun around, strode over to her bed and stripped off the quilt. Where did he get off, looking at her with those X-ray eyes? She made herself a cocoon of the quilt, the top edge rising above her ears and back of her head, leaving only her face peeking out. She wheeled around to face him.

"He came to apologize for yesterday. I was the perfect harridan to him, *if it's any business of yours,* which it isn't."

Alex took his hands out of his pockets and rubbed the back of his neck. "Okay. You're right. I'm sorry, it's really none of my business." He wandered over to her upright and looked at the music spread out on the top. The hands went back into his pockets again. He paced over to the sink and frowned down at the roses. Then he paced back to the piano and stared down at the keyboard.

"Okay," she said. "Out with it, before you wear out the rug."

He turned and faced her. "It's your business if you want to see this guy. I just hate to see an attractive, spunky, intelligent woman go around looking like a wounded doe because of some untalented creep with a good profile."

"Like a wounded doe?" she asked with echoes of disbelief.

"You know what I mean. Like yesterday. Delicate bones, huge eyes, camera in soft focus. Bambi after the hunters come."

"No, I do not know what you mean. And anyway, Bambi was a buck, not a doe," she said with a toss of her head.

He seemed to consider this. "Bambetta, then," he said at last, his eyes crinkling at the corners.

Good, he was back to comedy. "Bambetta? No, thanks. I think I'll go with Spunky."

"Well, Spunky," he said, "why don't you get dressed? It so happens I know of a place that's available, and I thought I could take you to check it out."

"Really?" She nearly lost her grip on the quilt. She hastily pulled the edges together again. "Where is it? How much are they asking?"

He backed toward the door. "Get ready first."

"Alex. Tell me." She stamped her foot, but to no effect. Her foot caught in the folds of the quilt and pulled it from her shoulders. She shrugged back into it.

Alex had the door open now. "I'll wait for you outside by my car." He went out into the hallway and closed the door behind him.

How completely maddening. Jo dropped the quilt and raced to her closet. Why wouldn't he tell her?

Alex leaned against his car and looked over at the entrance to Jo's apartment building. She'd be down soon if she dressed as quickly as she did everything else. He'd gotten out of there pretty fast himself. He had to. She'd flashed those brown eyes at him and played peekaboo with the quilt when he'd said he had a lead on a place.

He pushed off from the side of the car and paced the sidewalk. He'd nearly blown it then. He'd had to keep his hands in his pockets just to stop from reaching out to take her in his arms, quilt and all. All wrapped up, she was just as seductive as she had been standing in the doorway in that T-shirt thing, face flushed and ready to tear into Nick Keith.

He balled his fist and punched the palm of his other hand. That bastard. Showing up here with flowers. He should have broken his nose when he had the chance. Nick still had some hold on her, and the sooner Alex got her out of his reach, the better.

He stopped his pacing and leaned against the car again. Now came the tricky part. He was not going to be altogether truthful with her. Hell, he was going to flat-out lie to her. He rubbed the back of his neck. It was for her own good. No, he'd better not start lying to himself. The whole ruse was for himself, because she was becoming an obsession. What if he was right, and she was the one for him? He couldn't let this chance slip by.

He looked back toward the entrance to her building. She was running down the steps. She'd put on white jeans and a red top. Good, she'd left her hair down, though she'd brushed it. And she was carrying those damned flowers.

"Hi," she said, all pink cheeked.

"Hi yourself." He opened the passenger door and got Jo settled in her seat. Then he went around the car and sank into the driver's seat. She placed the flowers between them.

"Do we have to drive around all day with Nick Keith's floral offering?" he asked.

"Isn't that what they call funeral wreaths? That's sick, Alex. As a matter of fact, Spunky was hoping you'd drive by St.Joseph's Hospital so we could drop them off. Cheer somebody up."

He felt himself breaking into a broad grin. "Anything for Spunky," he replied.

The warm spring sun streamed through the windshield. The glass had intensified the warmth of the rays, making the closed car hot and stuffy. Jo poked at the window button. Alex turned the key so she could work the window, but didn't start the car.

He sat facing forward, hands on the steering wheel. This was the hard part. There was no script involved, just pure ad lib. "I have to tell you something." He paused, pushed his own window button and watched until the glass disappeared between the rubber strips.

"Yes, that's the way we do it on the soaps," Jo said. "You say—" she deepened her voice "—'Jo, there's something I have to tell you.' There's a three-second cut to a reaction shot of my face, then fade to a commercial." She slid down in her seat and put her knees up on the dashboard.

Okay, MacHail, just say it. The words wouldn't form in his mind. A cross breeze wafted through their windows and the scent of roses engulfed him. She had worn a red rose the first day he met her. Not a real one, though, like these. The sweet smell, the bright color, suited her.

"If it's something really big," she went on, "like 'I'm pregnant and you're not the father,' the next time you start to tell me you'll be interrupted by a phone call or by someone coming in the room."

He dropped his hands from the steering wheel and shifted around in his seat to face her. "I'm not pregnant," he said, straight-faced.

"Well, that's a relief." She grinned at him. "Out with it, then. I'm all atwitter."

Not true. She looked perfectly calm, with no sign of her usual jittery energy. She had curled up in the seat like a kitten on a warm windowsill.

"When I tell you about this place," he said slowly, "I want you to hear me out. Just consider the possibility and don't fly off the handle."

She turned her head so that her cheek rested against the upholstery and gazed up at him. "Why would I fly off the handle?"

"I don't know, but recent experience..." He left the sentence unfinished.

"Oh," she said in a little voice. "Right. I have been a bit touchy with you, haven't I?"

"Is that what you call it?"

"Okay, okay. I overreacted a couple of times yesterday. I had a bad day. I'll be good today." She traced an *X* on her chest. "Cross my heart. *Now tell me about this apartment . . . please?*"

He took a deep breath. "It's not an apartment. It's a house. My house. And I need a roommate."

Jo scooted upright in her seat, her eyes wide with surprise. "You what?"

"I recently bought a house, and I need to find a roommate, but I don't know how to go about it. I thought maybe we could solve each other's problems."

She shook her head slowly. "All other considerations aside, Alex, you wouldn't want me as a roommate. I do lots of work at home. And I play the piano a lot."

He'd ignore those "other considerations" and just go for the things he could argue with. "Exactly what I need." He leaned toward her. "I'm not home much. Right now I'm working twelve-hour days. Lots of weekends I have to go out of town on business. I don't want to leave the house empty too much."

"You could hire a security service," she said.

"A roommate would be more economical." He leaned back and rested his forearm on the steering wheel. "Besides, I need someone to look after my cat."

Jo shifted in her seat to face him. "You have a cat?"

"Do you like cats?" He mentally crossed his fingers.

"We always had cats when I was little. Not now, though. No landlord wants pets."

"This one isn't exactly a pet." He looked away from her and watched a car roar past. "He's a feral cat."

"Feral. You mean wild?"

"Someone must have dumped him when he was a kitten, and he survived somehow. I found him going through the garbage, and started leaving food out for him. Now he depends on me." He turned and looked straight into her eyes. "If he had to fend for himself again, I'm afraid the coyotes would get him."

"What do you mean, the coyotes? Where do you live, anyway, on the Rio Grande?"

"Vista del Mar. There are coyotes in the city, you know. They feed on house pets, especially cats. Just last week we found the carcass of one of my neighbors' cats," he said with just the right amount of regret.

Jo put her hand up to her mouth. "Oh, the poor thing," she breathed.

That had gotten to her. He pressed home his advantage. "Come look at the house first before you decide. It's a big house. You'd have your own bathroom. Pay the same rent you're paying now. Just see for yourself. Then we can have lunch and discuss all the pros and cons."

"Okay," she said. "I did promise to be nice today, didn't I? Let's go."

They took the freeway north along the coast. Nice that Alex didn't insist on carrying on a conversation. Jo just wanted to look. She kept her window open and breathed in the salt tangy air.

It would be wonderful to live near the ocean. Wait a minute—she couldn't really be considering Alex's offer. She was just going to look to be nice to him. He might think he needed a roommate, but she was really the least likely candidate.

What would his house be like? The ones along the ocean were perched precariously on the cliff edge, some even right above the high-tide line like death-defying high-wire acrobats.

They left the highway, turned inland and began to climb a winding road up into the hills that bounded the coast. She couldn't see any houses here, only mailboxes perched on wooden posts and narrow driveways half-hidden by shrubs.

Suddenly they turned on a tight switchback curve and the road, still climbing, headed them back in the direction of the coast. Where was this house, anyway?

Alex said, "Here we are." He turned up a narrow driveway that rounded one more curve before ending in front of a set of five double garages.

"Are these all for you?"

"No." He smiled. "Just these two. There are five houses up here." She got out of the car and looked up the hill. Now she could see the homes spread out in a random pattern, each one a different design but all clad in adobe-colored stucco and topped with red tile roofs. Arched entryways and occasional heavy beams evoked the architecture of early California.

Just past the garages, a flagstone path curved past a border of anemones and Iceland poppies. Jo followed Alex to the house. He unlocked the front door and ushered her in. This was not just another modern house like the ones she'd seen in the architectural magazines in the dentist's waiting room. Those all had white walls, white furniture and soaring spaces of profound impersonality.

This house had soaring spaces, too. The living room was nearly two stories high, but it wrapped her in warmth. Pale russets, creamy oranges and soft yellows flooded the room, overflowing from the walls to the plump sofas and chairs and onto the handmade rugs. This room would still be sunny on a rainy day.

Jo crossed over to one of the tall west-facing windows and looked out at the Pacific Ocean in the distance. Alex came and stood next to her. She turned to face him.

He tugged at his left ear. "Well?" he asked.

"I'm speechless."

He quirked an ironic eyebrow at her.

"You're right. I'm never speechless. It's beautiful, stunning, exquisite, charming."

"Does that mean you like it?"

It was her turn to quirk an ironic eyebrow. She hadn't imagined a house like this, but now she could see it was just exactly right for him. She turned to survey the room once more. A large collection of colorful masks hung on one wall next to an enormous flagstone fireplace.

"What are these?" she asked, pointing.

"Mexican dance masks."

"They're wonderful. You must have been collecting for a long time. You have so many."

He pursed his lips. "Actually, not so long. Many of them were given to me."

She sensed something unspoken there. "Get-well presents, when you broke your leg?"

He gave her a quick, hard look. "Yes, as a matter of fact," he replied in clipped tones. "How did you guess?"

Jo took a few steps toward the wall and examined one of the masks up close. So the broken leg was still off-limits. "Last night you mentioned that you learned Spanish when you were in the hospital in Mexico City." She spun away from the wall and gestured at the room. "The whole house seems to have a kind of Mexican feel. The colors are really warm. Was that your idea?"

"I knew what I wanted, but I had help from a designer. Let me show you the upstairs." He started for the staircase.

Jo followed him up carpeted stairs that switchbacked at a landing lit by long slit windows. "Remember you asked me a personal question last night?" she asked his back.

Alex turned around at the top of the stairs. "Yes, I remember."

She walked the rest of the way up the stairs. "Well, I have sort of the same questions to ask you. How could you afford this house? I know some actors are well paid, but..."

"I made some good investments." He walked on down the hall. "And I'm mortgaged to the hilt," he said over his shoulder.

Jo walked after him into the master suite. She'd guessed its huge size from seeing the floor plan downstairs. Just as in the living room, warm colors glowed from the walls and the Mexican textiles on the furniture and the floor. The room had the same wonderful ocean view, but evoked a simpler, more Spartan feeling.

"Nice," Jo murmured, then added in a louder voice, "Were those the investments you made instead of going to college?"

Alex flashed her a keen look that dissolved into a slow grin. "Some of them. I'll tell you about it someday." He

aused for a beat. "I'll talk about my investments and you'll
alk about how you support your widowed mother. Okay?"

So he *had* read the No Trespassing sign she'd put up last
ight. That made the score one-all in the figure-each-other-
ut game.

Alex stepped back into the hall and stopped by the door
f a small bedroom that had been converted into a mini-
ym and housed an array of exercise equipment.

"Ah, yes," Jo couldn't help teasing. "The household
hrine to the gods of physical fitness—Bulging Pectoralis
nd Flat Abdominalus."

"You're not into physical fitness?" he asked.

She shrugged. "I could never get used to working out on
nachines. What I really love is swimming. I go to the
MCA about twice a week and swim."

He led her down the hall to the last bedroom, this one
nfurnished. While nowhere as large as the master bed-
oom, it was still generously proportioned. Clerestory win-
lows lined the top of a long southern-facing wall, providing
oth privacy and ample light. And in the narrower, east
vall, a large moon window displayed the mountains behind
he house.

"Your bathroom is right across the hall. And—" he
valked over to a wall of louvered doors and pulled them
pen "—over here you have a large closet complete with
lrawers, shelves and racks as well as the usual poles for
anging clothes." He sounded as proud as if he had built it
imself.

Jo peered at the vast expanse of the closet. "I'm afraid
ny wardrobe would be a little lonely in there."

Alex's face fell.

Good heavens, she'd hurt his feelings. "That's a won-
lerful closet, a dream closet," she added quickly. "It's just
hat at the present I don't have a dream wardrobe." She
urned to face him squarely. "You're really serious about
his roommate business, aren't you?"

He folded his arms across his chest. "Completely seri-
us. I thought when you saw the house you'd be sold."

"The house is incredible." She looked from one wall to the other, measuring the distance with her eyes. "This room is almost as big as my studio. The closet is bigger than my bathroom. But, come on, Alex, you know I don't need anything fancy, I just need someplace to move into right away."

"So move in."

The midday sun slanted down onto him from the high windows, throwing his face into a relief of light and shadow. One ray in particular traced the stubborn line of his jaw. He looked like someone used to getting his way. Maybe she should try reasoning with him.

"Look, we hardly know each other."

"I'll be happy to provide character references. For my part, I'm a good judge of people, and I think we'd make pretty compatible roommates."

Jo walked over to the closet and inspected the shelves and racks. She couldn't really be contemplating this absurd offer, could she? No, of course not. It was just that Alex made everything sound so plausible. If he'd been selling encyclopedias, she'd have bought two sets by now. But living with him? She couldn't do that.

She opened and closed several drawers. Of course, she wouldn't really be *living* with him. He hadn't suggested anything like that to her. He hadn't even touched her. But twice so far, his looking at her had been like a touch—a warm, sensuous caress.

Suddenly she felt light-headed. She tottered and clutched at the side of the drawer.

Alex reached her side in two steps and put an arm around her waist to help her regain her balance. "Are you all right?"

He was touching her now, and she felt all warm and tingly where his arm rested. A nice feeling—too nice, considering the situation. Next thing she knew, she'd be leaning against that hard, muscled chest of his and tilting her head back and...

"Jo?" Alex asked, his face inches from hers.

She jumped back. What had gotten into her? "I'm okay,"
he said with a nervous laugh, "but didn't you say something about lunch? I'm starving. I missed my breakfast."

"Lunch. Of course. It's coming right up. Actually, we
have to drive down. I thought you might like a picnic on the
beach. Can you hold out that long?"

She nodded. She was just hungry. Why else would she be
having these weird fantasies? She was off men. Everyone
knew that.

Alex led the way back to the kitchen. Jo liked the friend-
liness of the room. Kitchen and dining room were both a
half level up from the living room. One long counter separated the kitchen from the dining area, which in turn opened
out over the living room.

"You can see the view from here," Jo observed.

"Let's go out the back way," Alex said. "There's one
more feature I want to show you." A door in the breakfast
nook opened up into the utility room.

"In-house washer and dryer. How nice." This was a selling point for sure. She'd spent way too many late nights at
the laundromat.

"It's convenient, but that's not what I want to show you."

Right outside the back door Jo saw a small bowl with a
few cat kibbles in it. "The feeding station for the feral cat?"
Jo asked.

Alex nodded. "But that's not it, either." He headed down
a flagstone path.

"Is he around? Can I see him?" She scanned the yard.
The back of the house was terraced to adapt to the gradual
grade of the hill. Redwood screen fences separated the
property from the neighbor's.

"He's mostly nocturnal and very skittish. I don't know if
he'll let you get close." He had reached the gate in the back
fence. He opened it and let Jo pass in front of him.

Jo walked down a few steps and then she saw it. "A pool!
You have a pool!" Now a pool could be a real temptation.

Chapter Six

The beach had that special freshness of early spring. The sun had heated the sand, but a swift breeze snatched at the warmth. Alex found a good spot, spread out a blanket and placed the wicker picnic basket in the middle.

Jo had been pretty excited about the pool, but he clearly hadn't won her over yet. Maybe the beach, or Lewis's lunch, would clinch it. He eased himself down next to the basket. Just keep acting the looking-for-a-roommate role and don't spook her—that should do it.

Jo stood nearby, sandals dangling from her fingertips, slowly curling her toes in the warm sand. She had pretty feet, dancer's feet—narrow with a high instep. He'd like to hold one of them in his hands and feel the soft skin of that curve, the fragile bones beneath.

The sun suddenly burned hotter, and the breeze couldn't cool him off. What was happening to him, anyway? He flipped open the lid of the hamper.

Jo stretched out on the blanket next to him and leaned back on her elbows. Her knit top pulled tight across her breasts. *Oh, God.* Alex quickly lowered his gaze and got

usy unpacking napkins, plates, glasses and the seemingly
endless array of food Lewis had prepared for him.

"What did you do, hold up the local delicatessen?" she
asked.

Alex had to clear his throat before he could make his voice
work. "A friend of mine has a catering business," he replied. "Let's see, what have we here. There's roast beef,
pâté, two kinds of cheese, baguettes and Dijon mustard."

He opened the containers and organized them next to the
basket. "Then there's three kinds of salad," he went on.
"Also Greek olives and cherry tomatoes for garnish. A nice
chardonnay to wash it down, and early strawberries to end
with."

"Looks good, but what are you going to eat?" Jo asked.

"That hungry, huh?" Alex handed her a plate and a large
piece of bread. "Go ahead, take what you want. I'll eat the
leftovers," he said, slipping in with her joking. He un-
corked the wine, poured some into two glasses and handed
one to Jo.

They sat facing the waves. The sun reflected off the restless water, and Alex squinted against the glare at wet suit-
clad surfers performing their feats of balance and agility on
the breakers. The breeze gusted gently from the ocean and
amplified the roar and crash of the waves.

Out of the corner of his eye he watched while Jo took
enormous bites from her sandwich. She ate with zest and
pleasure, like everything else she did.

She turned and looked at him. He quickly shifted his
gaze.

"Okay, MacHail, out with it," she demanded.

He turned his head to watch her. Her eyes danced. Just
sitting still, she sparkled.

"Out with what, Barnett?" he answered.

She popped the last bite of sandwich into her mouth and
held up her hand to signal him to wait until she'd swallowed it. "You're too quiet. You're holding something in.
That's bad for the digestion." She served herself some more
salad and began building another sandwich.

If he told her the truth, she'd run like a deer. "I'm jus
trying to figure out what the problem is with my offer."

She shrugged. "I just don't think you're being too ra
tional." She picked up a cherry tomato. When she sank her
teeth into it, the juice dribbled from the fruit. She licked the
drops from the corner of her mouth.

Not rational was right. And he was about to lose what bi
of rationality he had left. Wordlessly he handed her a nap
kin. She took it and dabbed at her chin.

"What's irrational about needing a roommate?" he asked
her. "I just want a compatible person to share my house and
look after my cat when I'm away. I think you're it." He took
a bite of his sandwich and took his time chewing it.

Jo lay down sideways and propped herself up with an el
bow. "Look, why don't you advertise and select somebody
compatible that way?"

"I don't have enough time for that." He opened the last
two containers. "Would you like some strawberries? Lewis
sent along some *crème fraîche* for dipping."

Jo reached over with her free hand and took a straw
berry. She dipped it in the soft cream, but instead of eating
it strawberry and all, she licked the cream from the berry
first, making little sounds of pleasure in her throat all the
while.

Alex averted his eyes. What would she think if he just ra
straight out into the ocean? A nice freezing dip would help
right about now.

She selected another strawberry and treated it like the
first. Then she sank all the way down on her side and
propped her head up with her hand. "You're not very typ
ical, are you?"

Alex put his unfinished sandwich down on his plate.
"What do you mean?"

"For one thing, most actors want to go from soaps to
movies, not the other way round."

Alex lowered himself onto his side, too, in mirror image
of Jo.

"I guess you're right. The truth is, I would have taken any role just to be working again."

Her eyes opened in quick surprise. Why had he said that? Now he would be in for it. She didn't know about Buddy. She'd think he was talking about his leg. He wasn't up for any "poor you and your shattered leg" pity.

"What's the other way I'm not typical?" he asked quickly.

She looked at him for a long moment. "Well, I was going to say ego, but I might change my mind about that if you keep asking me what I think of you."

"You think actors are pretty egotistical?"

"I think actors need strong egos because they have to deal with so much rejection in their line of work. But a lot of them just get inflated egos."

"Like Nick Keith?" he couldn't resist asking.

Jo rolled onto her back and shielded her eyes with her arm. "Ugh. The master creep. Wash your mouth out."

"Okay," Alex replied, buoyed by her response, and reached for the chardonnay. Jo's half-full glass rested in the sand nearby, and he added a splash to it. She still lay with her arm across her eyes. Her hair had fallen away from her face in a careless sweep onto the blanket, revealing one small, delicate ear. Alex could almost feel the softness of her earlobe between his lips and the sensation of matching its softness with that of his tongue.

Jo lifted her arm and turned her head toward him. "Well, can I?" she asked.

Alex jumped. "Sorry. I missed that. Can you what?"

She gave him a sharp look. "I said, can I ask a personal question?"

"Sure, ask away."

"What about your social life?"

"What about it?" he replied too quickly.

"Tsk, tsk." She waggled her finger at him. "You said I could ask."

He swallowed hard. "I don't have much of a serious social life. I've been pretty married to my career for the past ten years. Is that what you wanted to know?"

"No, but that's interesting. What I meant was, how would you feel bringing someone home, with me in the house? Wouldn't that be sort of...dampening?"

Alex shifted position slightly. Just having Jo in the house would be anything but dampening without anyone else in the picture. But he wasn't about to tell her that just yet. "I don't see a problem. What about your social life?"

Jo turned her face to the sky and folded her arms behind her head. "I think I might marry my career, too. Solve a lot of problems that way."

"Good. You and your career can move in tomorrow."

"Hold it. I didn't say anything about taking you up on your nutty offer."

Alex sat up. Why was she so stubborn? "It's a perfectly rational idea. Let's just talk about the practicalities. You have how long before you're out on the street?"

Jo consulted her watch. "Something over forty-eight hours."

"Right. So why don't you consider this a temporary shelter? Move in, but keep looking for a place of your own. If you find anything you like better, move out."

"What about you? What about your cat?"

"My cat and I are willing to take the gamble. Same rent you're paying now. Plus you get a cleaning lady that comes once a week."

"I'd share the cost of the cleaning lady."

He shrugged. "Whatever you say."

She slapped her hand down on the sand. "No. This is not going to work."

"You know what your problem is? You've got some phony idea about independence. You think that taking care of yourself means doing everything the hard way."

Jo sat up with a jerk. That had gotten to her. Alex lay back down on the blanket, feigning complete relaxation. Jo snatched up her glass and downed the remaining wine. She

leaped to her feet, stood downwind from Alex and brushed
the sand from her pants.

"Think I'll take a stroll along the beach," she told him.

"Think I'll take a little siesta," he replied. He rolled over
onto his stomach and closed his eyes.

Jo walked along the damp, firm track between the dry and
sea-soaked sand left by the now receding tide. Alex was too
perceptive for his own good. She broke into a jog and disrupted a convention of sea gulls. They lifted themselves
grudgingly eight feet off the ground and reconvened behind her.

Okay, make that too perceptive for her own good. He'd
hit the bull's-eye with that last remark. She used to drive her
mother nuts by always wanting to do everything her own
way.

Sandpipers, distracted from their search for sand crabs in
the wet ooze left as each wave retreated, raced ahead of her
on long stick legs. When she gained on them, they, too, took
off in brief flight. Why not let Alex help her? He seemed to
think she could help him, too.

Jo's calf muscles ached. Running on sand was harder
than it looked. She picked a spot about a hundred yards
ahead and forced herself to hold her pace until she reached
it. Then she stopped and gasped for air. Mindful of the wet
sand and her white jeans, she crouched down, balanced on
the balls of her feet, and waited for her heart rate to return
to normal.

What a great day this had turned out to be, after all. Alex
deserved the credit for it, really. She could be herself around
him, and not worry about fighting him off. Nick would have
had any woman in a half nelson before she'd finished her
sandwich and a full body pin not long after that.

Nick had turned her into such a cynic, she had trouble
seeing Alex for what he was—a basically honest and decent
man. He needed a roommate, and he thought she was the
perfect candidate. Why should she suspect his motives? It
was high time she put Nick behind her.

Jo inspected the damp sand in front of her. A seashell, a lone specimen amidst a strew of smooth pebbles, caught her eye. She picked it up and examined it. Conical and orange striped with a pearly luster on the folded-in side, it looked perfect. Then she spied the small round hole near the tip. No living creature hid inside.

She scooped up a handful of damp sand, placed the shell in the small excavation and carefully replaced the sand on top, patting it down. She looked around for a stick or large stone and spotted a gull's feather. She stuck the feather in upright as a marker, then stood and brushed the sticky sand from her palms.

Then, although each successive wave had been receding progressively farther and farther, one last large swell crashed in close to shore and poured its load of salt water and foam on the drying sand, swamping Jo's feet in its stinging cold. Surprised, she quickly back-stepped out of the water. When the tide sucked the water back out again, it bore away the gull's feather and left no trace of the miniature grave.

She walked back to their picnic spot. Alex was awake and sitting up.

"I saw you down there," he said. "Did you find something on the beach?"

"Spunky killed her evil twin, Bambetta."

"No kidding." He braced himself with his arms and rose to his feet. "Does that mean you're moving in?"

Jo nodded. "Remember what you said last night? That I had you mixed up with somebody else? You were right. Not every man is a liar. Just look at you. It's time I got over a few prejudices. So what do you say, roomie?"

Jo put out her hand. Alex grabbed it in a firm handshake. But why did he look less enthusiastic than she'd expected?

When Jo got back to her apartment late that afternoon she called her mother. She was out, but her sister begged to hear all about her new living arrangement.

"He's, like, only known you a week," Shelley breathed with a sixteen-year-old's enthusiastic diction. "And he asked you to move in with him? He must have really fallen for you."

"I'm renting a room in his house. We're going to be roommates, that's all."

"Hang on, Jo. Mom just walked in the door. Mom, you'll never guess. Jo is moving in with a man!"

Jo gritted her teeth. That Shelley, she'd wring her neck the next time she saw her. Kneeling by an open suitcase, she cradled the phone on her shoulder so she could pack and talk at the same time.

"Jo, dear? What's this Shelley's saying?" Her mother's voice sounded uncertain.

"Hi, Mom. I've got great news." She'd build it up for her. There was no need to mention the eviction. "I'm renting a room in a beautiful house in the hills above the Pacific Ocean. The house is owned by a really nice man I met at work. He's away a lot, and he needs someone to look after the house and take care of his cat."

"This isn't that Nick person, is it? You said you broke up with him."

"No, Mom. Nick is ancient history. This man's name is Alex MacHail. But it's not a romantic relationship. We're just going to be roommates, that's all."

There was a gap in the conversation. Was her mother even listening?

"I'm glad you found a nice place, dear. Excuse me a minute, will you? Shelley Ann Barnett, you are not leaving the house wearing that outfit! I'm sorry, Jo, but your sister insists that it is perfectly all right to go out wearing only underwear. Excuse me again, will you?"

The clatter of the phone being put down was followed by raised voices in the background. Then her sister got on the line.

"Jo? It's me. Will you please tell Mom that a bustier is not underwear. Everyone wears them."

"I'll tell her no such thing. Guess what? Even in L.A. you don't see that many bustiers." Jo put her meager collection of lingerie in one corner of her suitcase. A bustier, for heaven's sake. Shelley had grown up, and she hadn't even been there to see it.

"Look, can I stay with you this summer? I can't stand it here anymore. Mom is always going on at me."

"No, you can't stay with me this summer. You need to find a summer job, and you have a better chance there in Kansas City."

"Puhleeze, Jo. I'm sixteen, and I've never gone anywhere or done anything. Mom treats me like I'm five."

Jo could picture her sister's pleading expression. She had always felt more like a mother than a sister to Shelley, and she had trouble saying no. "Let me get settled into my new place and then I'll see about a short visit," Jo told her.

"I knew you'd let me. Gotta go. Bye." A loud clunk made Jo pull her ear away from the receiver.

"Jo, are you still there?"

"Yes, Mom, I'm here." Jo leaned her back against her now empty dresser and switched the phone to her other ear.

"Shelley is such a handful these days." Her mother heaved a sigh. "She just runs wild and I simply don't know what to do half the time."

"Isn't it normal for kids to want to assert their independence?"

"*You* were never like that."

True, but Jo hadn't felt she had a choice. Her childhood had ended at age ten when the life-insurance money had run out and her mother had started working double shifts waitressing.

"Let her have her fun. She's going to have plenty of responsibilities soon enough. Look, Mom, I have a lot of packing to do. I'll call you after I get settled. Okay? Love you. Bye."

An hour later Jo sat amidst the packed cartons and stared at the phone. Why couldn't her friends be as easily convinced as her mother? Each one had given her a different kind of protest about her new living arrangements.

From Sandy: "You are obviously looking for a place in the *Guinness Book of World Records*. You go out with this guy *one day* and he asks you to move in with him. What do you mean, you're just friends and you like it that way? Are you out of your mind? Alex MacHail has to be the sexiest hunk alive."

From Fran: "Please don't rush into anything. I know you're still hurting about Nick. You know you could always stay here until you find a place."

From Ed: "Why do you think I'm going to start saying things about the lady protesting too much? You need a place, and he needs a roommate. If you say there's nothing going on, then there's nothing going on. But if you expect me to believe that nothing is going to go on once you move in, then you probably also have a bridge you want to sell me."

Jo nested her few pots and pans for easier packing. She hadn't been very realistic, had she? They would be around each other every day, eating meals together sometimes, relaxing around the house on a weekend morning, sleeping at night in their separate rooms.

Ed was right. It would be naive not to expect a certain intimacy to grow between them, a friendly intimacy that might, in an unguarded moment, develop into something else. And what would that something else be? Alex had made it clear that he didn't want any serious involvements. His career was his wife. So any intimacy that happened between them would be nothing more than a sexual relationship of convenience on his part.

As for her part, she wanted nothing to do with any relationship, committed or noncommitted. After Nick, she'd stopped looking for the rainbow at the end of the storm.

The phone rang. She picked it up. "Hello."

"Hi." The voice was easily recognizable.

"Hi, Alex."

"What's wrong?"

"Nothing. That is..." She trailed off.

"Sounds like you're having second thoughts."

"I've been telling my friends, and they, that is, one of them thought..."

"Who?"

"Well, Ed."

"He thought you shouldn't move in?"

"No. He just pointed out that..." She cleared her throat. How could she phrase this? "That living together could lead to a kind of situation of intimacy."

"What the hell is a 'situation of intimacy'?"

"It's, you know, sex...um, a sexual relationship." Her voice was stupidly breathless. She had to get a grip.

"Of course," she said, "they, I mean Ed, wasn't even taking personal taste into consideration. I mean, not everyone is attractive to everyone else, are they? Simply because they happen to be together a lot, or not a lot, but say on a regular basis, someone you don't find attractive in that way isn't suddenly going to become attractive, are they?" She sounded so stupid. Alex would think she was an absolute idiot.

"Come on, Jo. You've put me in the middle of a mine field. I step one way—I'm a lech. I step the other way— you're ugly."

"Maybe I didn't phrase it quite right, but I think I have a point here," Jo persisted.

"All right, in the interests of fairness, tell me what you think. And be honest."

"It's not the same thing."

"You're waffling."

"Okay, okay. Speaking as honestly as I can, I'd have to say that you are, objectively speaking, an attractive man." An understatement, if ever there was one. She flashed briefly on the scene at his house, his arm around her waist and she feeling all warm and tingly.

"So it's nothing against you." She rushed on. "But I'm not sexually attracted to you. I'm just not the kind of person who can separate her hormones from her heart, and at

this point both systems have shut down for the duration."
She really did sound as if she was protesting too much now.
But it was the truth. Wasn't it?

Alex remained silent. Why didn't he say anything? "Was
that honest enough for you?" she asked.

"Admirably honest."

"So what do you think?" she prodded.

"I think we'll have to trust each other. You tell me if I
make you uncomfortable. I'll do the same. Okay?"

He made it sound so simple. Well, maybe it was. "Okay."

"Good. Now, I got in touch with a friend of mine. He's
an experienced mover. He has access to a truck, and he has
a helper. So we should be able to move everything, even the
piano."

Here he was taking over again. She'd already called about
a rental truck and contacted the piano movers. "Thanks,
but I want to get piano movers. I know my piano doesn't
look like much, but it has beautiful tone. I'd hate to dam-
age it."

"George knows what he's doing."

"How do you know?" she asked, building up steam. "Do
you know anything about pianos?"

"No, but if you hum a few bars I'll fake it."

She'd forgotten he had a stand-up routine. "That joke is
so old it's bald."

"No, it's so old it's on Medicare," he said.

"No, it's so old it's in the Smithsonian," she returned.
That stopped him.

"So I'll see you tomorrow morning," he said.

"See you."

Jo hung up. Almost immediately, the phone rang. She
picked it up, and before she could say anything, Alex said,
"It's so old they found it in the Dead Sea Scrolls."

"You've got to think of the comeback line at the time, not
later. That's how the game goes."

"There's something you should know about me. I believe what matters is whether you win or lose, not how you
play the game."

Chapter Seven

Jo felt a bright warmth on her lids and slowly opened her eyes to the sunshine pouring in through the round window. This was heaven. Alex could have his view of the ocean; she got the morning sun.

She shifted her head on the pillow and took in her new bedroom. Everything was in place. Alex's friend and his friend's helper had conducted the move with the efficiency of an army on military maneuvers. Her piano, all her electronic equipment, even her mismatched collection of dishes had arrived intact. She had spent yesterday evening unpacking, hooking up her computer and rearranging her furniture.

She gazed out the window at the coastal mountains and the blue sky beyond. She had put the bed in exactly the right spot. How long had it been since she'd seen anything but the stucco wall of the next-door apartment building when she looked out a window?

Jo threw off the covers and jumped out of bed. She'd lolled around long enough. Today was going to be a work marathon to make up for the time she had taken off to move. But work would have to wait until she had her morning swim. Jo shrugged out of her nightshirt and stepped into her black tank suit.

Talk about dreams come true. She now had her own pool. Well, almost her own. Alex said the owners of all five houses on the hill shared it, but didn't use it very much. She bet no one used it at six-thirty on a Sunday morning—at least, not until now.

Jo opened her door carefully and eased out into the hall. Good roommates didn't make noise early on Sunday mornings. Stepping into her bathroom, she picked up a towel then took care to be quiet all the way downstairs and out the back door. She paused by the cat's now empty dish. Alex really ought to put water out, too.

She hurried the rest of the way along the path, out the gate and down the steps to the pool. After dropping her towel onto a patio chair, she stepped to the edge of the deep end and dived in. She swam as far as she could underwater, then, lungs bursting, she surfaced. This was great, perfect, stupendous.

"Yahoo!" she yelled. Heavens, what was she doing? Jo clapped both hands over her mouth and let herself sink below the surface. If she woke the neighbors she'd get herself thrown out her first day here. She pushed off from the bottom and struck out in a crawl.

After the first few lengths, swimming became hypnotic. Jo gave herself over to the rhythm of her breathing and the regular movement of her arms and legs. The cool water on her skin energized her, yet the familiar sensation of weightlessness soothed her. How lucky to have this paradise all to herself.

She felt a surge of water push against her side, signaling that someone had just dived into the pool. So much for solitude. With the next turn of her head for air she glimpsed the swimmer two lanes over, a man with long brown hair. It had to be Alex. She kept on swimming, but her rhythm was broken. She tried, but couldn't regain her trancelike state.

Jo did five more laps, then gave up. When she reached the end of the pool she grabbed the edge and blinked a few times. Alex stood in front of her on the cement deck. She looked at his feet through chlorine-blurred eyes. Not just his feet, but his lower legs, too, and the right one had a vivid red scar that went from knee to ankle. Was that the "broken" leg?

That was no simple break. What had she learned in Red Cross training years ago? Compound fracture? Whatever it was called, it looked major. And the scar was nasty, too. No wonder he was so touchy about it. Not wanting to get caught staring, she dipped back under the water, then resurfaced with her head tilted back, letting the water sweep her hair from her face. She kept her gaze directed at his face and smiled up at him.

"I didn't expect to see anyone else out here this early on a Sunday morning," she told him.

He returned her smile. "There's nothing like a swim to start off the day," he said, rubbing one arm briskly with a towel.

Her gaze followed the passage of the towel up his well-muscled arm, over his broad shoulder to his equally broad and muscled chest. Whoever had invented the term *hunk* must have had Alex MacHail in mind.

"Need a hand up?" he asked.

She refocused her eyes on his face. He looked at her with blue, amused eyes. Oh, my gosh. She'd been staring, and he knew it. How embarrassing.

He slung his towel over one shoulder, bent and held out his free hand in a silent offer to help her out of the pool. She'd been climbing out of swimming pools unaided her whole life, but why be rude and point that out? She curled up her legs, braced her feet on the rim of the gutter and grabbed Alex's hand.

He gave a hard pull, and she surged out of the water and onto the cement deck very fast—too fast. She put out her free hand to stop herself from crashing into him. Her palm flattened against his chest, and she came to a stop just inches away from him.

"Whoa, there," Alex said, steadying her by her elbow.

She smoothed the flat of her hand over the soft hair on his chest with its rock-solid layer of bone and muscle just beneath. His heart beat double time against her palm. Her own heart pounded in an answering rhythm. The early morning wrapped them in silence, the only sound the thudding of their hearts. Then a sparrow tweeted noisily in a nearby hibiscus bush and rustled out of the leaves to fly over the fence.

Jo snatched her hand away and took a step back. "Sorry," she said. "I didn't expect you to pull so hard. I don't think you know your own strength." The air chilled her wet skin and raised goose bumps. She clutched her arms across her chest and shivered.

"Maybe," he said. He picked up her towel from one of the patio chairs and draped it around her shoulders. "But you're still the gold medalist in swimming." He turned toward the path back to the house.

Jo fell in step beside him. "No, I'm not. I just love the water. And swimming is such a great way to burn off excess energy."

He held the gate open for her. "So how many laps does it take to rid yourself of the excess?"

"I don't keep count. I just swim until it feels right." Today, though, she hadn't burned off any at all. Her restlessness had something to do with touching Alex's chest, feeling his heart and her heart beating together. But she wasn't about to tell him that. She didn't want to think about it too much herself. Roommates, that's all they were, just roommates, and she'd better not forget it.

They passed the cat's dish. "You know, Alex, you should put out a water dish for the cat. He's probably drinking from the pool, and that's not good for him."

Alex made no reply. Jo flashed him a quick look out of the corner of her eye. She had to squash the urge to look at his chest again. She'd better not look at him at all until they were both dressed. "Think I'll take a shower." She walked ahead of him through the back door and hurried through the kitchen to the stairs.

"I'll put on some coffee," Alex called after her.

The sunlight fell across the breakfast table in a warm parallelogram. Jo took the seat opposite Alex and broke the sun's bright symmetry on the surface of the table. With the warmth of the window-filtered rays on her head, her just-washed hair would dry quickly. She took a sip of coffee.

Alex looked up from his newspaper. "If you don't like conversation in the morning, tell me. I'll observe the hour of silence."

Jo put her coffee mug down. This was more like it—no more hearts pounding unexpectedly, just two roommates chatting over breakfast. "There is no time of day I don't like conversation. My mother claims that when I was little I would talk for hours in my sleep." Jo shifted in her chair and looked out the sun-filled window. "Actually, it just occurred to me that I might become agoraphobic here."

His brows came together in a worried frown. "Isn't that when people are afraid to go out of their houses?" he asked.

"I was using the term very loosely. You know, fear of open spaces. I'm not used to so much space, or seeing the outside world." She gestured toward the window. "Here, the outdoors comes indoors and gets you."

"I know what you mean." He rested his forearms on the edge of the table and leaned forward. "My first day out of traction, they took me outside in a wheelchair. I'd been in this little curtained-off space for a month. The corridor seemed a mile long. And being outside was incredible. It was as if I had never really looked at the sky before."

So he could talk about his broken leg, after all. It sounded like a pretty harrowing experience.

She looked at him closely. His long hair hung loose. Even only half dry from the sun-warmed air, it was still thick and shiny, and somehow tempted her to touch it. Maybe the softness of it around the sculpted bones of his face made it so attractive. Or, more likely, any hairstyle would look good on a man this handsome. He'd probably tie it back when it had dried. She lifted a testing hand to her much longer hair. Hers was half dry, too. Then a strong suspicion struck her.

"You were in the hospital for a month, you say? And it would have been a long time after that before you were able to work, right?"

"Months," he admitted with a bleak look. "Why?"

"You haven't been exactly honest with me, have you? Right from the start, I'd say."

"If you'd tell me what you're talking about, I'll try to be as honest as possible." His voice sounded huskier than usual, and he seemed to be having trouble meeting her gaze. She had him on this one.

"Your hair must have grown inches since you stopped filming." She pointed an accusing finger at him. "It was never in your contract. You just said we couldn't cut your hair because I picked on that, didn't you?"

He sat up straight and looked right at her. "A nun in the hospital practically shaved my head. My director thought we were going to get back to filming fairly soon, so he put that rider in my contract." He held up his right hand like a witness being sworn in. "Honest, I didn't lie to you," he said. "I didn't lie to you about that," he repeated himself.

Alex put the wicker picnic basket down so hard on Lewis's stainless steel counter that the pastry chef gave a jump and squirted whipped cream garnish in the wrong place. Lewis and his three helpers turned from their tasks on the other side of the large kitchen and looked at him.

"Sorry," Alex said to the pastry chef. She nodded to him and went back to piping out decorative designs onto strawberry tarts.

"I brought your basket back," he called.

Lewis came over to the counter and picked up the basket. "What's the matter?" he asked. "Didn't she like the lunch?"

Alex slumped down on his usual stool. "Like it? She loved it. She ate most of it herself. She eats like, like..."

"Like a horse?" Lewis filled in for him. He walked over to a row of open shelves and slid the basket into its place.

Alex looked at Lewis in surprise. "No," he protested. How to explain that Jo enjoyed eating? She savored her food. And when she was hungry, she, she...ate like a horse.

"Well, yes," he admitted. "But what I meant was..." The image of Jo, head tilted back, taking small licks of cream with the tip of her tongue flooded his memory. A rush of desire swamped him. He scrubbed at his face with his hands. He had to stop this.

He lowered his hands. "Forget it," he said with a sigh.

"So did it work? Is she going to move in?" Lewis asked.

"She moved in yesterday."

"You don't sound too excited. I thought that's what you wanted."

"I did want it. I still want it. It's just..." Alex slipped off the stool and paced back and forth. "For the time being we're just roommates. Plus she's got a thing about being lied to."

Lewis pursed his mouth. "Unusual trait in a woman."

Alex stopped pacing. "You can cut the sarcasm. I'm just saying she's more sensitive about it because of that jerk she used to see. So she's suspicious."

"Of you? Come on, she's got to know you're a straight arrow."

Alex didn't reply.

Lewis narrowed his eyes and said, "Okay, what'd you do?"

Alex straddled the stool and leaned his elbows on the counter. "I convinced her I needed a roommate to help take care of my cat when I go out of town."

"You don't have a cat."

"Yeah, I know."

Lewis looked at him thoughtfully for a moment, then gave a dismissive wave of his hand. "Don't worry about it.

She'll come around. She must like you or she wouldn't have moved in.''

Alex nodded. "I think she likes me, but that's not what she says." He paused and waited while the pastry chef picked up the tray of decorated tarts and put them in the refrigerator. When she was out of earshot, he went on. "She brought up the topic of us becoming more than roommates already."

Leaning closer to Lewis, Alex lowered his voice. "Only she put it like I might get sexually interested in her, just because she was around. Not knowing that I'm interested day and night already. And she tells me, no way is she interested in me."

"She said that?" Lewis asked.

Alex nodded. "But I think she's already interested. She just doesn't know it yet."

"I'll buy that. But if that's the case, why aren't you with her now? It *is* Sunday. I thought only us poor caterers had to work on Sundays."

"She has to work today, too. But we did go for a swim this morning, around six-thirty."

"Six-thirty? Swimming? You?" Lewis stared at him, incredulous.

"Yeah, it was great."

Lewis shook his head in wonderment.

His friend didn't understand, but Alex wasn't about to explain how he had deliberately pulled Jo out of the pool so she'd bump into him. She hadn't stepped back right away, either.

"She works. You leave," Lewis said. "This isn't going to get you very far."

"I was thinking maybe—dinner?"

"Dinner, of course. The lady likes to eat, and I just happen to be doing a very nice dinner tonight for the Hoopers." He walked to the end of the counter, picked up a thick black notebook and brought it back to Alex. He flipped through several pages.

"Let me see. We have a choice of entrées. Either chicken or fresh tuna, both grilled with citrus. Then there's white beans with ham, cilantro and mint. Or you could have anchovy potatoes. Also roasted red bell peppers with basil, very tasty. Tomato and olive salsa. Salad of apple, feta cheese and spiced pecans. And to go with it, a very nice 1986 Johannesburg Riesling. What do you think she'll like?"

"I think you'd better give me everything."

"Now, how did I know that's what you were going to say?"

"And could we have one of those strawberry tarts? I'd like to torture myself some more."

"You what?" Lewis asked.

"Forget it."

Lewis looked at his watch. "Come back around three, and I'll have it ready for you."

"Thanks. You're the greatest. See you later." He turned to go.

"Wait," Lewis said.

Alex turned back, eyebrows raised.

"You forgot to tell me. What'd she say when you told her about Buddy?"

Trust Lewis to bring up the tough subjects. "I haven't told her yet."

"What?"

"The timing's not right."

Lewis put his fists on his hips. "Hold it. You're worried about the cat you don't have, but not about letting her know you're adopting a kid?"

Alex shifted his feet. How could he explain it, even to Lewis? He rubbed the back of his neck. "I'm worried about that, too, but I want to make sure of her first. Win her over."

"And I think you're making a big mistake. Tell her up front."

Alex shook his head. He'd never get the words right. This chance had come along, and he didn't want to blow it. If he was right about them being perfect for each other, she'd understand.

Alex slowly straightened his leg out on the couch. He could barely make out the shapes of the living-room furniture in the dark, but he didn't feel like turning on any lights. As soon as the cramping in his leg eased he'd go back upstairs and give sleep another try.

Dinner had gone pretty well. It had been short, though, because Jo had had to get back to her computer and finish working. He'd held back, kept things neutral, and she'd relaxed. She wasn't so suspicious now, ready to jump on the least thing. She liked him. He could tell. And somehow he'd find the patience to wait for her to realize she more than liked him. She couldn't spend every evening working. Maybe tomorrow night would be the right time to work on romance.

He cocked an ear toward the sound of bare feet padding across the hall. Maybe tonight was the time, after all. Should he make a noise or call out?

The small light over the stove came on, and from where he sat in the lower level of the living room, Alex could see Jo's head and shoulders as she moved around the kitchen. She got a glass, went to the refrigerator and poured herself some milk. So, she was having trouble sleeping, too.

The phone rang. Jo gave a startled jump, but recovered immediately and quickly picked up the receiver of the wall phone.

"Hello?" she said softly. Then she asked, "How'd you get my number, Nick?" Irritation was plain in her voice.

Alex swung his leg partway off the sofa. That jerk, calling her here. He started to get up then sank back onto the cushions. What could he do? She didn't even know he was in here.

"I'm sorry if someone left garbage in your driveway. It wasn't me, and I didn't send any flyer out."

She tapped her fingers impatiently on the counter while she listened to Nick talk.

"Yes, I wrote it. But I only showed it to one person. It was a joke, that's all...."

"No, everything's not a joke to me. Take split ends, for example. They're no joke. If you don't get them trimmed, your hair can split all the way—" She jerked the receiver away from her ear. "Nice talking to you, too," she said to the air. She reached over and hooked the phone back onto the wall mount.

Alex deliberately cleared his throat and watched her turn her head in his direction.

"Alex?" she called.

"I'm in the living room. Sorry to eavesdrop. I thought you were raiding the refrigerator, and didn't want to disturb you."

She picked up her half-finished glass of milk and walked down the few steps to the living room. Even in the faint light from the kitchen, he could see her clearly. She must have been able to see him, too, because she came right to the sofa and sat on the other end. He shifted his leg a little to give her enough room.

"I thought you were asleep," she said. "I was afraid the phone would wake you. Guess you heard." She drank the rest of her milk and put the glass on the coffee table.

"I woke up a little while ago. Why didn't you hang up when you heard who it was?"

"Why hang up when I can enjoy such scintillating conversation and get hung up on myself? Was it your leg that woke you up?"

Alex looked at her more closely in the faint light. "Yes, as a matter of fact. Did you really enjoy the conversation?"

"I'll give you two aggies for your glassie."

"I think I missed something there."

"Didn't you ever trade marbles? That's what we're doing. Sort of. Actually, we're trading secrets, which is better. Only one stipulation. No backsies."

"What's that?"

"What kind of childhood did you have, anyway? That means no going back on the agreement once you've said you'll trade. Does your leg keep you awake often?"

He looked at her for a beat. "Okay. I'll trade. But remember, no backsies. You want to know if my leg keeps me awake?"

"I want to know why every time it comes up, I get a big No Trespassing sign. It hurts right now, doesn't it?"

Here they were, sitting on the couch together in the middle of the night, and she wanted to know about his leg. He sighed.

"See? That's what I mean," she said. "You agreed to tell. So talk. Where does it hurt? Why does it hurt?"

"Sometimes it hurts where the docs put it back together with a bunch of metal, but most of the time it's the torn muscles and tendons that act up. I have to work out to build the muscles up again. They get sore, too."

"Wait," she said. "I have an idea." She grabbed one of the throw pillows, put it on her lap and slid over toward him. "I do a terrific massage."

Jo put her hand on his ankle and Alex automatically tensed his entire body. Things were going faster than he'd expected.

"It's okay, really," she said. "I promise I won't hurt you."

Wasn't that supposed to be his line? He let her lift his leg and lower it onto the pillow on her lap.

She fingered the hem of his pajamas. "Nice. What is it? Silk?"

"My mother always gives me a pair for Christmas." He wouldn't tell her just yet that he didn't normally bother with pajamas.

She stroked with firm pressure down the sides of his calf. It did feel good. There and elsewhere.

"I used to rub my mom's legs and feet when she got off work. She worked as a waitress, and her legs were always sore."

He couldn't believe it. She really meant to give him a leg massage—and that was all. All he had to do was relax and not enjoy it too much. "You were pretty young, weren't you? You said your father died when you were nine."

"Looking back on it, nine does seem really young. But at the time I thought I was almost grown up. My sister was a baby, and I pretty much acted like I was her second mother."

"You like kids?" He tried to make his voice casual.

She peered at him in the dim light. "You mean generally, or for myself?" Then she went on without waiting for an answer. "Of course I like kids. I feel like I've already had a family. I still get roped into parenting problems when I call home. But children are a big responsibility. No one should have kids without thinking and planning really hard ahead of time."

This was the moment. He should tell her about Buddy now. But what should he say? *You know, I have a kid?* Or, maybe—*speaking of children, I have one of my own.* He opened his mouth, but no words came out.

"We've gone off the track," Jo said. "It's still your turn. Why don't you want to talk about your leg?"

She never gave up, did she? "I don't like the way people react," he said. "First pity for being crippled. Then praise for being someone you're not. 'You're so courageous to go on. How brave of you to fight against the odds.' As if I had a choice."

"I know what you mean. That's how people talked about me taking care of my sister while my mother worked. And about me supporting them now. 'You're a brave girl,' or 'You're such a good daughter.' They don't get it—when you care, it doesn't feel like a choice."

"You do what you have to do, that's all," he said quietly.

"Exactly." Her hands stilled on his leg. The warmth of her fingers came to him through the thin material. He gazed at her shadowed face, at her dark eyes glinting in the dim light. She understood. She'd been there herself since she was a kid. And he'd known—how, he couldn't guess—but he'd known. She was perfect—pretty, sexy, funny and she understood. He couldn't lose her.

Did she feel it, too? The connection between them? It was difficult to tell, but there was no time like the present to find out. He lowered his leg to the floor and pulled the pillow from her lap to his own. "Your turn," he said, patting the pillow.

"Wait a minute," Jo protested.

"No backsies, remember? Now just put your feet up here, and I'll give you a relaxing massage."

Jo turned sideways on the sofa and obediently placed her feet on the waiting pillow. Alex cradled a foot in one hand and rubbed her instep with the other. Her foot felt just as delicate and her skin as smooth as he had imagined that day on the beach.

"Mmm," she murmured. "That does feel good." She nestled against the cushions and closed her eyes.

Alex slid his hands up to her ankle and massaged it with gentle pressure. He'd rub her calf muscles next, then her knee. His heart thudded in his chest. If only she'd open her eyes and look at him, he'd know if he was going too fast for her. Or if she wanted him to pull her onto his lap and kiss her as much as he wanted to.

"Jo?" he said softly.

"I know," she said without opening her eyes. "It's my turn. Ask away. I have no private life where Nick is concerned, anyway. The gossip mill at the studio made sure of that."

Hell, how had Nick come into this? They'd broken up—why couldn't he stay out of her life? Okay, he'd play. Maybe she was still hung up on the jerk. He had to know where he stood. "Why didn't you hang up as soon as you recognized Nick's voice?"

She opened her eyes and looked at him thoughtfully for a moment. "It's hard to explain without sounding downright perverse. Giving Nick a hard time is my one bad habit. I know I shouldn't do it, but I can't resist. It's like when you have a scab, and you know you shouldn't pick at it, but you pick at it anyway.''

"If you pick at a scab, you'll make an old wound bleed again," Alex said.

"That's right. It's a good reminder. Better than tying a string around your finger."

"Reminder for what?"

"Not to fall in love, of course."

He moved his hands back to her instep. This was going to take a little longer than he'd thought.

Chapter Eight

The motif of the Bach prelude chased itself from one end of the piano to the other like a soprano and a baritone playing a game of echo. Jo sat a little straighter, raced to the end, then dropped her hands to her lap. Maybe she'd sped up the tempo too much there at the end, but it was notated allegro vivace. Just like her life.

What a hectic week. When had she had so many rewrites to do all at once, on top of the regular scripts? And her car had let her down again, the day after she got it out of the shop. Lucky she had Alex as a roommate. She could always drive to the studio with him. Of course, she had to get there at the crack of dawn and stay late, but she didn't mind.

Didn't mind? Face it. She liked it. This roommate business had turned out a whole lot better than she'd imagined. She and Alex had become friends. Sometimes it even seemed that something stronger than friendship lurked just below the surface.

Jo stood abruptly. These kinds of thoughts always made her feel antsy. She didn't want to get involved with anyone, and neither did Alex. So she'd just put it out of her mind.

She marched over to her computer and gazed down at the screen. A twinge of pain shot up the back of her head. She rolled her head around and rubbed the back of her neck. She'd spent too long at the computer this morning without a break. Playing the piano usually relaxed her, but not this time. All the muscles in her neck felt as if they were tied in knots.

She glanced at her desk clock. Good grief, what had happened to the morning? She had a story conference this afternoon, and if Alex was going to get her to the garage to pick up her car first, she'd have to hurry. Maybe she'd better check with him. He might've changed his mind about driving her in on his day off.

She hurried into the hallway and toward the stairs. What was that clinking noise? She shifted direction and followed the sound to Alex's minigym. Sure enough, he was working out, sitting on the side of the massage table, his ankle hooked to some pulley gizmo that clinked every time he straightened or bent his leg.

She stood in the doorway, transfixed, while he slowly raised and lowered his leg, his eyes closed in fierce concentration. He wore only shorts, and a sheen of perspiration bathed his body. He gripped the edge of the table and strained all his muscles with the effort of moving the weight on the pulley. She should leave and come back, or maybe clear her throat. She shouldn't stand there and stare. But she couldn't help herself, she really couldn't.

Dark curly hair spread across his chest, then narrowed to a line that disappeared in a very interesting way into his shorts. Her hand tingled with the memory of touching his chest that one time by the swimming pool. What would it feel like to explore that fine line of hair? She pressed her fingers over her mouth. That was just the kind of thought she'd better avoid.

Alex lowered his leg with one final clink and opened his eyes. His gaze met hers square on. "Something wrong?" he asked.

She slid her hand from her mouth, to her chin, to her chest. "Uh, no." How intelligent. She sounded like a cavewoman. No wonder, she *felt* like a cavewoman—her whole body tingling with animal attraction while she stared at his shoulders, his chest, his stomach—whoa, stop right there. She had to get control of herself.

Alex leaned forward and unfastened the ankle cuff that linked him to the pulley. "You want to go pretty soon?" he asked. "Pick up your car?"

Yes, that was it. She knew she'd come in here for some reason. "I'm ready whenever you are." She rubbed the back of her neck. Her head hurt, that was her problem. She couldn't really think straight.

Alex picked up a towel and rubbed his face and torso. "I just have to shower. It won't take me long."

"You know, if you'd rather not drive in, I'd understand. It is your day off." She held on to the back of her neck and rotated her head.

"Turns out I have to go in anyway. So it's no problem." He dropped the towel on the table. "What's the matter? Got a sore neck?" He moved toward her.

She quickly dropped her hand. "Just a little stiff, that's all. I sat too long at the computer without moving." She took a step backward.

"Wait," he said, holding out his hand. "Come back here. My physical therapist taught me a great neck release. It'll fix you right up."

That sounded like a good idea. Too good, really. "That's okay," she said, but didn't move away. Her voice sounded tinny in her ears, like a bad long-distance connection.

Alex beckoned to her with his hand. "Trust me. I don't do any of that bone-cracking stuff. I let you massage my leg, didn't I?"

True. And then they'd traded off. The feeling of his strong hands had stayed with her, too. And that wasn't all, if she was honest with herself. A longing for more touching everywhere had drifted over her when she wasn't expecting it. But that wasn't part of their roommate deal.

Alex pulled a straight-back chair away from the wall. "Come on. Sit down."

She did as he said. Alex stood directly behind her. Jo tensed in anticipation of his touch. He gently brushed her long hair from her neck over the front of one shoulder. She shivered with pleasure.

"You all right?" Alex's husky voice seemed deeper than usual.

"Tickles," she lied, glad a curtain of hair shielded her face.

He rested the palms of his hands on her shoulders and with firm pressure stroked his thumbs down the nape of her neck, hitting every knot. She closed her eyes and groaned.

Alex's hands stilled. "Does that hurt?" he asked.

"Hurts nice."

He repeated the same firm strokes several times. She pressed her lips together and tried not to moan from the pleasure of it. Her neck muscles untied themselves under the heat and pressure of his hands, and her other muscles slowly released their tension.

His fingers moved from her neck to her shoulders. A wonderful languor slowly seeped through her.

"How does your neck feel now?"

His hands rested quietly on her shoulders, their warmth heating her skin through her T-shirt.

"Very relaxed."

"You shouldn't work such long hours," he said.

"It's your fault, you know."

He lifted his hands from her shoulders. "How's that?"

Jo twisted in her chair and looked at him over her shoulder. "Didn't they tell you? Viewer response to Johnny has gone through the roof. It usually takes a couple of months to build such a positive reaction to a new character. Remember that when your contract comes up for renewal." She stood and faced him.

He picked up the chair and placed it against the wall. " will, but how does that affect you?"

"Viewers want more of Johnny—so we have to give them more. That means new scenes, and rewriting the current script to make the new ones fit in. Didn't Ron tell you any of this?"

"Andy called and said I've been scheduled to shoot more days, but he didn't say why. That's why I'm going in this afternoon."

Jo shook her head. "He's not called Rotten Ron for nothing." She gave him a straight look. Alex might be too nice for this business. "Don't let him use you," she warned.

"Don't worry. I won't." He gave her the full impact of his blue gaze. "Your neck all right now?" he said huskily, more to his question than the simple words.

He knew what she'd been thinking, feeling when she walked in and saw him—he had to. He stood there, waiting. The moment hung between them, full of possibility. He could reach out his hand. She could take one step closer to him. He could wrap her in his arms.

He didn't move and neither did she. Disappointment pricked her. She dropped her gaze.

"My neck's fine now," she said with forced perkiness. "Feels great, very loose." She rotated her head in demonstration. "Thanks."

"You're welcome." Alex picked up his towel from the massage table. "I'll be ready in a few minutes and we can go." He headed out the door, and all the trembling possibilities of the moment went with him.

Jo followed the curving flagstone path down to the garage. The bright spring sun gilded the anemones and Iceland poppies lining the pathway. Alex had said he'd be right along, but she felt too jittery to wait for him in the front hall. Maybe she could think more clearly out in the fresh air and golden sun.

It didn't take an advanced degree in interpersonal relations to see what was going on. He wouldn't have offered to rub her neck if he didn't like her. And she wouldn't have let him, if she didn't like him. Like him—such a good old euphemism for something else. It hardly covered what she felt while staring at Alex's body. That was more than liking. But how much more?

Of course, nothing had happened. Nothing overt, anyway. But they'd been close to something there. She hadn't imagined that. And something probably would happen before too long. If she wanted it. Did she want it? Wasn't she the one who'd vowed no more men, especially no more actors? But she'd never met anyone like Alex when she'd made that resolution.

She reached the garage and fished in her purse for her keys. She'd never had a garage before, either, much less one with a fancy automatic opener. Alex usually did this, but why shouldn't she have a turn? She fitted the barrel-nose key into the lock panel to one side of the garage door. With a clank and a whir the garage door slowly raised itself upward.

In addition to his car, his side of the garage was piled high with large cartons and variously shaped objects covered with old sheets. She'd noticed before that he barely had room to park in here. What was all this stuff, anyway?

Jo sidled into the narrow space on the side of his car, twitched one corner of a sheet and peeked under. There was a brand-new mattress and box spring still in their original plastic wrapping. Next to that was a dresser in some light-colored wood. It looked new, too. She couldn't get any closer to the other things. One large, rectangular carton said only Twin Size on the outside.

"Jo?" Alex called from the open garage door.

"Right here," she said, backing out along the cramped space next to the car.

"What are you doing?"

She hadn't heard that sharp edge in his voice before. She glanced at him quickly. Did he think she was prying? "Just looking at all the things you've stored in here. There's hardly room to park. What is all that stuff, anyway?"

He looked down at his key ring and spent a while searching for the right key. "Just old furniture the decorator said wouldn't go with the new pieces."

Jo bit her lip and half turned away. That furniture was new, never out of the store cartons. Why would he lie about that?

He crossed to the back of the car, unlocked the trunk and loaded a leather suitcase inside.

"Are you going somewhere?" Jo asked, staring at the lid of the trunk as he closed it with a thump.

He turned to her, but didn't quite meet her eyes. "Yes. A business trip. I had planned on going next weekend, but with the new shooting schedule, I moved it up to this one. I'm leaving right from the studio."

He sidled into the garage and got in on the driver's side. She moved to one side to let him back out. What was going on? First he doesn't tell the truth about the furniture, then he's going out of town without any warning. Okay, he had mentioned business trips before. That's one reason he'd wanted a roommate in the first place.

Alex stopped the car next to her and she got in. He let the car idle and turned partly toward her in the seat.

"I'm sorry I didn't mention going away sooner," he said. "I only got the call about the changed shooting schedule a couple of hours ago."

"That's all right," she said. "Your trusty roommate will take care of the house and the cat."

He said nothing, but stared out the windshield. Finally he spoke. "I'll miss you, roommate."

"Jo, I need to see you a moment," Linda called from her strategic location behind her desk.

Jo turned and headed back toward Linda. What now? She halted in front of Linda's desk.

Linda handed her some preprinted forms. "You need to fill these out right away."

Jo looked down at the papers. "What is this?" Another memorandum from Ron? She doubted it. She could do no wrong in Ron's eyes today—the Johnny story line had already boosted fan response.

"Change-of-address forms, of course. You should have filed them with personnel right away. And I have to keep my Rolodex up to date, too."

Jo took the pen Linda offered her and bent over the desk to write.

"I heard you moved in with Alex," Linda said. "Pretty fast work."

Jo gritted her teeth. She would not respond to Linda—no matter how much she provoked her. In fact, it was time Linda learned a little accountability.

She lifted her head and looked Linda in the eye. "A week ago Thursday I had important phone messages. I never got them."

"That's terrible," Linda said, staring back at Jo. "You know, sometimes people are careless and reach into the wrong box. I bet someone else picked up your messages by mistake."

How long could Linda hold that unblinking stare? She was trying for wide-eyed innocence but looked like a snake instead, a lying snake. Maybe threats would work.

"I hope no one gets careless again, or I'll have to bring it up to Ron." Jo lowered her gaze and continued to fill in the blank spaces.

"I'm sure that won't be necessary," Linda replied. "But tell me about your whirlwind romance with Alex. I couldn' believe my ears when I heard."

Jo sighed. Other beings needed food and oxygen to live. Linda needed food, oxygen and gossip to live. And maybe judging from how underweight Linda always looked, maybe she didn't need food, after all. "I was evicted from my apartment, and Alex coincidentally needed a roommate. I'm renting a room in his house, period."

Linda raised her eyebrows in disbelief. "You expect me to believe that you're just friends?"

The elevator doors opened behind Jo. Out of the corner of her eye she saw Ed step out. Reinforcements, at last. She had to get away from Linda's prying. "Yes," Jo said firmly. "We are friends, and that is all. And I don't intend to discuss it again."

Ed joined her in front of Linda's desk. "Wanna bet?" he asked, his cynical grin well in place.

He was a big help. Jo handed the completed forms to Linda, who gave her a bright smile.

"Okay," Linda said, leaning forward in her chair. "You're just friends, but you must know him pretty well by now. So what's he like? You know what I mean—what's he really like?"

Where did people like Linda come from? Was there some special training they underwent to make themselves particularly dense and insensitive? "Well," Jo said slowly. "I don't know if I should say this in front of Ed, because this really is girl talk. But there are two very unusual things about Alex." She bent toward Linda.

"First, for an actor, he has a small..." She held up her thumb and forefinger about an inch apart. "A very small...ego."

Linda frowned and blinked her eyes, but Jo gestured for her to move closer and said more softly, "Second, he has a big, and I mean really big—" Jo dropped her voice to a whisper "—collection of Mexican dance masks."

Linda sat up straight with a jerk and pursed her mouth like someone who'd bitten into a lemon. You'd think anyone who hated being made fun of as much as Linda did would learn when to back off.

Jo held up her wrist and looked at her watch in an exaggerated gesture. "Will you look at the time? I can't stand here gossiping all day." She turned to Ed, who had the expressionless look of someone trying hard not to laugh. "Shall we see if Fran has arrived yet?" she asked him.

They strolled down to Fran's office but found it empty.

"Might as well wait here," Ed said, and settled into his usual chair. "I think you have now earned a permanent place in Linda's bad graces."

"Good." Jo put her briefcase next to the desk and sat down. "I consider that a worthy achievement. She's a sure one for my short list if she screws up my phone messages again."

The door opened and Fran stepped into the room. "Don't tell me you two are already hard at work," she said.

"We're hardly at work, as you well know," Ed replied. His smile for Fran had none of its usual cynical twist.

Fran dropped purse and briefcase on her desk and sank into her chair. "I've been meaning to ask you, Jo. How are things going with Alex?"

It was the very question she'd been asking herself since Alex had dropped her off at the repair shop. She still didn't have the answer. Maybe she didn't even want to know. Jo looked at her watch to avoid Fran's gaze. "Don't we have a story conference right about now? Are we ready to face Bea with our latest?" She glanced up and caught Fran and Ed exchanging knowing looks, then turning to her with their eyebrows raised. She never got away with changing the subject around these two.

"Don't look at me like that," Jo said, leveling a look at each of them in turn. She swiveled her chair several times, swinging her legs in a restless half circle. "Everything's fine. Alex is very nice, very easy to be around." Except for making her mind go soft around the edges with thoughts of touching him, of being caressed in turn—but she didn't have to tell them that.

"Everything's fine," Ed said. "That's great. Then why are you so nervous?"

"Me nervous? What are you talking about?"

"Jo," Fran said, "you're not very good at hiding your feelings. We don't want to pry. But we're your friends, and if this arrangement is creating problems for you, we want to know."

The scene in Alex's garage played out in her mind for the umpteenth time. Her living arrangement wasn't the problem—she was. She could be falling for Alex in a major way, and he had lied to her. Maybe Fran and Ed could help her understand, because for the life of her she couldn't figure it out.

"I like Alex. We've become friends—I think." She caught Ed's sardonic look. "I know it sounds fake, but it's true. We've gotten to know one another, you know, talked about our lives. But this morning Alex drove me in to pick up my car. I went down first and opened the garage, and you'll never guess what I found."

Ed held up a warning hand. "Never challenge me like that. Let's see, we're playing What's in Alex's Garage and I guess—eight hundred thousand back issues of *National Geographic.*"

Jo shook her head. She should've known better than to try to have a serious conversation with these two.

"No?" Ed straightened in his chair. "How about his adored Shetland pony he had stuffed when it died?"

She'd just wait him out.

"That's good, Ed," Fran said. "But I think it was a collection of life-size, anatomically correct, blow-up dolls and their designer wardrobes." She looked first at Ed, then at Jo. "I win, don't I?"

Jo rubbed her temples. Her head hurt again. "Anybody have an aspirin?"

"I'm sorry, Jo," Fran said. "I got caught up in Ed's game. Ed, don't start teasing again. Jo wants to talk to us."

No, she didn't. How could she explain when she didn't understand herself?

"Jo started it," Ed said.

"Now stop that," Fran ordered. "Come on, Jo. Tell us what was in Alex's garage."

"Furniture. What I saw was bedroom furniture. All brand-new."

"Yes?" Fran nodded, encouraging her to go on.

"And when I asked Alex about it, he said it was old furniture the decorator had nixed for not fitting in with the design scheme."

"That's it?" Fran asked. "That's all?"

"He said it was old when it was new," Jo said.

"What? Do you think he's a fence for furniture thieves?" Ed asked.

"Come on. I'm trying to explain. He acted funny when he said it."

"Probably wondered what you were doing going through his garage," Ed said.

Fran nodded in agreement. "You like him, don't you?" she asked.

"Maybe more than like," she admitted.

"Then take it slow. If you're worried about him not telling the truth, take it very slow."

Jo trotted down the stairs to the studio, holding pen and notepad in one hand and skimming the metal banister with the other. What did Andy need from her? He'd been unspecific on the phone. Please don't let it be another rewrite this late in the afternoon.

Alex would probably be in the studio now. Was that why she was nearly running down the stairs? Was she so eager to get just a glimpse of him? She couldn't be that hopeless—could she?

She pushed open the fire door to the hallway. Alex stood leaning against the yellow cinder-block wall, one leg bent-kneed, the sole of his shoe resting against the wall. He looked up at her from the script he held open in one hand. "Hi," he said with that slow smile of his, and pushed away from the wall.

Jo's heart beat faster than the dash down the stairs warranted. "Andy sent for me. Some problem with a script, but I don't know what." She was jabbering. She needed to slow down. Forget about Alex and simply do her job. She moved past him toward the door to the main studio.

"Andy's busy. Said he'd be out in a minute. They're all rushing around in there, trying to shoot extra scenes."

Jo turned back toward Alex. "If anybody can do it, Andy can. He's a terrific director. Perfect for this business, because he never wastes any time."

The double doors to the studio opened with a crash and Andy came striding toward them on his long, sticklike legs. "All right, children, what's the problem with this scene?" he asked in his very British accent, and peered at Jo over his beaky nose.

"That's what I'm waiting for you to tell me," Jo replied. "I still don't know which scene we're talking about."

"The scene where Johnny—" he gestured to Alex "—rescues Lorna from the gang of young toughs."

One of the metal doors opened a little and a production assistant stuck her head into the hallway. "The lighting's fixed," she said to Andy.

"Right-o," he replied. "Explain it to her, Alex. We'll be ready to block the fight scene in ten minutes." The assistant pushed the door farther open and let Andy through. The door closed behind them both with a clunk.

Jo uncapped her pen and held it poised over her notepad. "There's a script problem with the fight scene?" she asked. "Is it a dialogue problem?"

Alex faced Jo and leaned one shoulder against the wall. "It's the scene between Johnny and Lorna after he chases the gang members away."

The pen wavered. He meant the scene where Johnny kissed Lorna. It had been her idea, and everyone agreed she'd hit on the perfect way to heat up the tension between Lorna and Johnny—and give the fans what they wanted. She looked down at her notepad and drew a squiggly doodle. "So what's the problem?"

"It's not exactly a problem. I'm just not too clear about how I'm supposed to play it. We're under so much pressure right now, we don't have a lot of time to rehearse, or try different things."

Jo glanced up at Alex, then down at her pad again. The squiggle acquired a number of elaborate loops. "Okay, it goes like this. Johnny is attracted to Lorna, but hasn't admitted it to himself. They're usually in conflict because she keeps trying to get him to make up with his dying mother."

"Also he has this inferiority thing, because of his limp, right?"

"Right."

"So why does he kiss her?"

"Why?" He made it hard for her to concentrate. She couldn't even quite remember how the scene went now. She stuck her pen behind one ear and held out her hand. "Let me see the script for a minute."

He placed the script on top of the notepad. She curved her fingers up and over to anchor it in place and leafed through it with her free hand. "Okay, here's the place." She ran a finger down the page, scanning the words. "He wants to show her she should be more careful. Not frequent the rough neighborhoods."

"He kisses her to show her she should be more careful?"

"Sort of. Lorna claims she can take care of herself. So Johnny grabs her to show her she's vulnerable. But once he touches her, he can't resist—the attraction is too great."

"I'm still not too clear. Maybe it would help if you could run through the scene with me."

"Run through . . . I couldn't do that. I'm a writer, not an actor. Big difference."

"Just talk me through the scene, Jo. Otherwise I'll be here all night doing retakes."

"Talk? Okay, I can do that."

"Good." He pulled the script from her hands and dropped it on the floor.

Jo took a step back. Hadn't he just said they'd talk? He moved toward her, and she found herself backed against the wall.

He grabbed her upper arms above the elbow. "Johnny grabs Lorna, right?"

She nodded in reply. The warmth of his touch, his very nearness made it hard to think of words.

He relaxed his grip and slid his hands slowly up to her shoulders. "Once he touches her, he can't stop himself." He slid his fingers along her neck, cupped her cheeks in his palms and brought his face within inches of hers. His gaze dropped from her eyes to her mouth.

Jo held her breath. He wouldn't actually kiss her, would he? This was just rehearsing—wasn't it?

"He kisses her," Alex said. He touched his lips to hers, the merest brush of a butterfly's wings.

She leaned toward him, toward his teasing mouth, longing for more, hoping for kisses she hadn't let herself wish for, but had wished for anyway.

"The question is," Alex said, his lips barely touching hers, "does she kiss him back?"

He pressed his mouth against hers then, softly at first—a question, a tentative inquiry. She leaned closer and answered him in her own unspoken language. He pressed his lips firmly to hers then, moving his mouth subtly, knowingly. She slipped into a melting mindlessness.

The studio door opened with a clang and a production assistant said something, then the door clunked shut. Jo pulled back slightly and blinked to focus her eyes. Alex gave her his high-voltage smile, which was nearly lethal at point-blank range. His hands still cradled her face, and he stroked her cheeks with his thumbs.

"I have to go," he said, not moving.

"Oh?" She nearly whimpered.

There was something in his eyes. Regret? No, that was her line. He was holding back, like when he'd told her the furniture was old.

"I'll see you Monday. Right after work." He bent and kissed her lightly on the tip of her nose. Then he disappeared into the studio.

Jo sagged against the wall, fingers pressed to her mouth. Alex had kissed her. She dropped her hand to her side. Or had that been Johnny?

Chapter Nine

Night had blackened the living room windows. Jo shifted in her chair, pulled a pillow onto her lap and pushed the Rewind button on the VCR. She really should go to bed. Alex had been gone only twenty-four hours, and somehow her whole routine had fallen apart. She hadn't gone for a swim this morning. She hadn't taken Sandy up on her invitation to hit that hot new club tonight. And here she was staying up far too late. Why was it so hard to maintain her normal schedule? She pointed the remote at the TV and pushed the Play button. She'd go to bed right after she watched this scene one more time.

Jo tucked her feet under her and rested her chin in the palm of her hand. Alex appeared on the screen, clad in a T-shirt and tight jeans. It was Alex, and yet it wasn't. He'd developed a whole set of gestures for his role as Johnny, like shifting his shoulders around inside his shirt, and he'd made himself look like a bodybuilder, even though he wasn't.

The scene cut to Tracy playing opposite Alex as Lorna. She made an unconvincing social worker with her blond mane of hair and tight-fitting suits whose hems ended several inches above her knees. Jo pushed the Fast Forward, and Tracy's video image raced around the screen like a frantic mouse. She'd just get past Tracy's part before she started thinking too much about the scene they'd shot yesterday, and Alex kissing Tracy.

She fast-forwarded Tracy out the door and clicked the remote for normal play. The camera caught Alex in a close-up. She pushed the freeze-frame button and slid farther down in the chair, pulling the pillow from her lap to her chest. Alex stared out of the TV screen to a point just past her right shoulder.

Everybody commented on how gorgeous he was, but did they also see the essential niceness in him? Or how funny he was? Or how smart, for that matter. They had to know he was a fantastic actor. Look at what he'd done with this little part—vulnerability peeking through his tough-guy front with every movement. He could break your heart with that limp alone. Probably every female fan from here to Wichita wanted to take him home and kiss it to make it better.

Jo hugged the pillow and cradled her cheek on her shoulder. He'd kissed her and she'd felt better than she had in months, years—maybe her whole life. But was it real, or make-believe? Had he kissed her on impulse, or had he planned on doing it? She jabbed at the Off button and jumped to her feet. She had to stop making herself crazy thinking about it, and wait until Alex came home. Once she saw him again, she'd know where she stood.

Jo straightened the cushions on the chair, crossed the room and closed the television cabinet. Time for bed, but maybe she'd have a snack first. She headed for the kitchen, switching off lights as she went. What should she eat? She stood in the darkened kitchen and let the night silence fall around her. Suddenly she cocked an ear at a strange scratching sound. It was the cat, of course, the feral cat who came out at night, and now she would finally get to see him.

She tiptoed into the laundry room and peeked through the windowed panel in the back door. In the dim light from the walkway night-lights she could just make out an animal shape hunched over the food bowl. Pretty big cat. Wait a minute, that was no cat.

She reached for the switch by the door and flipped on the full outdoor lighting. The creature jerked its pointed nose out of the bowl and darted its head from side to side. She got a glimpse of beady eyes reflecting red as it turned its head into the light.

A possum, for heaven's sake. She jerked the door open. "Shoo," she said.

The possum looked at her, but didn't move away.

"Shoo," she repeated, and stepped outside.

The possum stood its ground.

She stamped her feet and clapped her hands. The possum turned slowly and waddled down the path. She stood in the doorway until it squeezed its round body under the gate and disappeared from sight, then stepped back into the house and shut the door.

Feral cats, coyotes and now possums. What was this, anyway, a nature preserve? She stood by the door and watched for several minutes, but the possum didn't return. That poor cat might not be getting much food. Maybe Alex would have a solution. She'd ask him about it, first thing, when he got home.

Jo backstroked lazily, squinting up into the glare of the late-afternoon sun. Alex was coming home tonight. That was all she'd been able to think about the entire day, even at work. Fran and Ed had been nice about her lack of concentration, teasing her in tandem, of course. Those two were so perfect for one another. There had to be a way to bring them together.

Jo rolled over and swam to the edge of the pool. If Ed would only say something, give Fran some clue about his feelings. She pulled herself out of the pool, grabbed her towel and hurried back toward the house. When she reached the back gate, the phone rang, the electronic beep faint in the distance. It was still ringing when she let herself in the back door. What was wrong with the answering machine?

She picked up the kitchen phone. "Hello?"

After a significant pause a woman's voice asked, "Who is this?"

Talk about no manners. "Jo Barnett speaking," Jo replied.

"I'd like to speak to Mr. MacHail."

"He's not here. May I take a message?" Jo searched around the counter for a pad and pencil.

Another long pause. "Are you a visitor there, or...a resident?"

Jo shivered and clutched her towel more tightly around her. "I live here, but whatever you're selling, I'm not buying. Alex might. Do you want to leave a message?"

"Have you been a resident for very long?"

What was with this woman, anyway? Sounded as if she was checking up on Alex. Could it be an old girlfriend? "Why don't you just leave your number for Alex?"

"Tell him to call Eunice Weeks as soon as possible. It's very important," she said.

Jo scribbled "Eunice Weeks" on a scrap of paper. "I'll make sure he gets your message," she said. "Goodbye." She hung up the phone and pushed the note into the middle of the counter.

She hurried upstairs to her room, stripped out of her swimsuit and reached into her underwear drawer. Empty. She'd forgotten that most of her lingerie was still in the laundry room. She wrapped her towel around her sarong-style and went in search of clean clothes.

The dryer disgorged its load of white and pastel shirts, shorts, socks, bras and panties—and one black item. Jo picked it up. It was a pair of Alex's briefs. Black—and sexy.

The phone rang. Jo padded into the kitchen and picked up the receiver. It had better not be Eunice Weeks again.

Alex closed the front door quietly behind him. Should he call out and let Jo know he was back? No, that would be too much like "Honey, I'm home," even though that was exactly what he wanted to say.

Pausing in the front hall, he heard Jo's voice in the kitchen. "That's terrific news. Thanks for everything you've done."

A few strides took him right through the kitchen doorway. Jo stood holding the phone in one hand and a piece of black cloth in the other. The towel she'd wrapped herself in barely spanned the crucial distance from breasts to top of thighs. If he was dreaming, he didn't want to wake up.

She stared at him with those doe eyes of hers, and bit her lip. He must've startled her coming in like that, but she looked glad, too—her cheeks all pink and her eyes were shiny. She couldn't be as glad as he was.

"I have to go now, Mr. Gomez," she said into the receiver. "Thanks again." She hung up the phone. "Alex...I didn't expect...you're home earlier than..." She clutched at the towel.

He'd definitely flustered her. "There was no traffic from the airport," he explained. No need to mention how he'd broken the speed limit most of the way home—thinking about seeing her, though never imagining this.

"Great, great." She nodded a couple of times and shifted her weight back and forth from one foot to the other. "Good trip?"

"Very good. Thanks." Plus the usual heartbreak of leaving Buddy behind, but he wouldn't go into that right now. "So that was Mr. Gomez on the phone? Your old tenants' association lawyer?"

"You'll never guess what he told me," she said, and stopped shifting her feet. "The judge ruled in our favor. We get back the rent money we put in that special account because Cranshaw Construction didn't help us find new housing. The money is such a windfall for me. I don't know what I'll do with it."

"If you're going to be walking around like that, maybe you should invest in a bigger towel," he teased.

She clutched at the towel even more tightly, if that was possible, and gestured with the hand holding the black cloth. "Please, no jokes. I'm embarrassed enough already."

"What is that?" Alex asked, pointing to the cloth in Jo's hand. From where he stood, it looked a lot like a pair of men's briefs.

Jo looked at her hand. "I spoke too soon. *Now* I'm embarrassed enough—more than enough." She held out the briefs. "These are yours, I believe, and don't look at me like that. I'm not into anything kinky. They got left behind in the dryer and I didn't notice when I put my clothes in."

What did she mean, don't look at her like that? He couldn't stop looking at her if he wanted to. And he didn't want to. Those eyes, those bare shoulders, the soft swell of her breasts against that impossibly titillating white towel—all compelled him to look, to more than look.

He put out his hand as if reaching for the briefs, which she still held out, and took her hand instead. Her eyes widened at the contact of skin to skin, but she didn't resist when he pulled her toward him.

"Alex?" she said breathlessly.

"How've you been?" he asked.

She gazed back at him. Drops from her wet hair dribbled onto her shoulder and coursed down the shadowed space between her breasts.

"Fine, just fine." She tucked a wet strand of hair behind her ear with a jerky movement. "I've just been for a swim. Haven't had my shower yet. That's why I smell like a swimming pool."

"Eau de Chlorine, my favorite scent." He bent toward the side of her head and sniffed. "It always reminds me of you." He picked up a strand of her hair and lifted it to his lips. "So you've been lolling around in the swimming pool all day?"

"And worked eight hours, too," she said in a rush, her eyes wide. "Not to mention that I ran interference for you with Eunice Weeks."

Alex dropped the strand of hair and straightened with a jerk. Mrs. Weeks. The adoption agency. "What did she want?" he asked urgently.

Jo narrowed her eyes. "My social security number and three references. Who is she, anyway?"

"She didn't say?"

"My guess is that she's been trained in intelligence gathering in areas of national security, but I could be wrong." She pulled her hand from his and crossed her arms. "You're not an undercover agent for the FBI, are you?"

"Did she leave a message?"

"Yes. She said for you to call, that it was very important."

Alex checked his watch. He might catch her if he called in the next few minutes. He looked up at Jo. He'd waited all the long hours of the return flight to see her—he didn't want to walk out on her now. But what if Mrs. Weeks had some new information?

"So go call her," Jo said and turned away from him toward the laundry room. "I'm taking a shower as soon as I get my clothes out of the dryer."

Alex stood in front of his bedroom windows, the phone cradled on his shoulder. The sky had darkened perceptibly in the long minutes he'd been on hold. Images of Jo wrapped in a white towel kept surfacing in his mind. She was a woman to come home to, he had no doubt about that. More than that, she *was* home. No matter where he went, if he was without her, she'd draw him back, the way the moon was drawing the surging waves of the ocean right now in the distance beyond his windows.

There was a click on the phone line and a clipped voice said, "Eunice Weeks here." She wasn't so bad in person, but always managed to sound so cold on the phone. No wonder Jo had been put off.

"Mrs. Weeks. Hello, it's Alex MacHail. I got a message that you called. Something new?"

"Yes, there is. Just a minute, let me get the file."

He'd never get used to the clutching feeling in his stomach when he had to face news about Buddy. His worst case of stage fright, doubled, was easier to handle. So many strangers held his future in their hands and acted as if they had the rest of their lives to get on with it.

"Here we are," she said. "Good news, actually. U.S. Immigration has approved your application for a visa for Alejandro."

Buddy's visa, at last. His stomach unknotted several notches. "Great. How'd you find out? I thought I'd get something in the mail."

"You'll be getting something in a few days. I called to see if I could prod them a bit, and it turned out they'd already acted on your application."

"Thanks for taking the trouble. I appreciate it."

"No problem. Sometimes they need to know that they can't take their own sweet time over these matters," she said in an unusual outburst of feeling. "Now you have completed all the requirements at this end," she added, back to being businesslike.

That was good news, but not good enough. "What's the situation with the Mexican adoption services?" he asked.

"They requested Spanish translations of your home study. I sent them off yesterday."

"But we asked if they wanted translations months ago and they said they'd do the translating themselves."

"Yes, I know. But they changed their minds."

Alex sank onto the side of his bed, shoulders slumped. Every time he turned around he faced a new requirement or had to file papers in yet another place. They never asked for anything unreasonable in itself, but all put together it felt like an endless paper chase.

"You know," Mrs. Weeks said, "I have a friend who's good friends with someone at the Mexican consulate here in Los Angeles. Maybe I can talk to her about your situation."

He sat up straight. Mrs. Weeks had never before suggested any action that didn't go strictly through channels.

"Thank you. I'd appreciate anything, anything at all you could do. If you'd seen Buddy's face this time..." He paused and cleared his throat. "I don't know how many more times I can go down there and not bring him back with me."

"You call him Buddy?"

"Alejandro goes by Buddy now. It's a nickname I gave him, and it stuck."

"I see. Well, I'll do my best. I know you'd make a wonderful father for Ale—for Buddy, and I don't understand why this process should be dragged out any longer."

She paused. She didn't usually hesitate over anything. "Was there something else?" he asked.

"Yes, one small matter." She paused again. "When I called earlier I spoke to a woman who said she was now residing there."

"That's right. Jo Barnett. She gave me your message as soon as I got in." She'd sent other messages, too, standing there with droplets falling from her hair onto the tops of her smooth breasts. He stood suddenly and paced as far as the phone cord would let him. "Is it a problem that she's living here?"

"In your home study interview, you said you had no emotional involvements with anyone and wanted to proceed with the adoption as a single parent."

"That was true at the time. But now I've formed a serious attachment..." What was he going on about? He was starting to sound like Mrs. Weeks. "I mean, I've fallen in love with a wonderful woman."

He'd never said it before—that he loved Jo. Not even to himself. It sounded good—it felt good, too.

"So this is a serious relationship?"

"Very serious."

"Are you planning marriage?"

"Yes." Now that she mentioned it, he did plan on marrying Jo. Why not own up to it? "But I still want to proceed with the adoption as a single parent. We haven't set a date yet. And I don't want to have to change any of the affidavits at this point. It would only delay things more."

"I believe you're right about that. Very well. We'll continue as we have been. My congratulations to you and best wishes to your fiancée. Goodbye."

"Thanks. Bye." He hung up the phone. What had he done? He'd lied to the social worker who was helping him adopt Buddy. Well, it wasn't exactly a lie. He wanted to marry Jo. He knew that. But what did Jo want? That was what he had to find out.

He found Jo filling the cat dish outside the back door. She'd taken her shower in record time, the way she did everything. No sense of fuss about her, but she'd put on lipstick and a loose kind of dress without sleeves that clung to her body one second then fell away when she moved.

He leaned against the jamb of the open back door. He could never be bored around her. Just watching her shake out the kibble enchanted him. She knew he was there, watching—her sideways glance gave her away. She straightened and took her time folding the top of the cat-food bag.

"While you were gone," she said, finally looking at him directly, "I found a possum eating the cat food. Do you think there's some kind of platform we could construct that a cat could climb and a possum couldn't? Because I'm not sure your cat gets very much of this food."

That damn cat. Well, he'd asked for it, hadn't he? But he could tell her the truth now. He had to. He couldn't tell Eunice Weeks he loved Jo and not tell Jo herself.

He pushed away from the doorjamb and held out his hand to her. "Come here."

Jo walked slowly toward him, clutching the cat-food bag to her chest with both hands. She stopped right in front of him and gazed at him warily. Was she afraid of him? No, that couldn't be. Jo wasn't afraid of anything.

He took the cat-food bag from her grasp and tossed it through the open door behind him. Without anything to hold on to, Jo clutched her hands together in front of her, and resisted for just a second when he took them both into his own. She had wonderful hands, broad palmed and long fingered. They looked superb racing over the piano keyboard. How would they feel touching his body?

He gripped her fingers and raised them to his lips.

She tensed, but didn't pull away. "Alex?"

"Mmm?" He turned one of her hands over, caressed her palm with his thumb, then placed a kiss where the life line and the love line joined.

"What are you doing?"

"I'm kissing your hand. Do you like it?"

"You know I like it. But why are you doing it?"

"Because I like it, too."

Now she did try to pull away, but he held her hands firmly and wouldn't release them.

"Jo, please. Don't run away."

She stopped trying to tug her hands from his. "I don't want to run away. I just want to know what's going on. The other day you said you wanted help with a scene, and you ended up kissing me."

"You kissed me back, I believe."

"Now you're kissing my hands. I don't understand. Are you teasing me? Or is this real?"

"Very real. As real as it gets," he answered.

"What about being roommates?"

"I never wanted a roommate. I just wanted you. You getting evicted was the luckiest thing that ever happened to me."

"What about someone to watch the house when you're away? What about feeding your feral cat?"

"There is no cat. I made that up."

"You what?" She jerked her hands from his and took a step back.

"I invented the cat. I wanted you to move in here, so I made up a story I thought would convince you. I was pretty sure you'd run if I told you the truth."

"And what is the truth here?"

"I care about you. I fell for you the first day I met you."

"Oh, please, we're not rehearsing a scene now."

"Don't talk like that, Jo. These are my real feelings. And if you were honest, you'd admit that you have feelings for me, too."

"I do have feelings. I have very strong feelings for someone who was warm and kind and liked my jokes, someone who confided in me, someone who teased me and kissed me and knocked me for a loop. But now I'm not sure that person exists."

"He exists. He's right here."

"No. You lied to me and you manipulated me. You didn't have to trick me into liking you. But you probably had your eye fixed on another goal—like taking me to bed."

"It wasn't like that. I simply wanted to give you some space away from Nick. You were hung up on him, and there wasn't room for anyone else."

"You're wrong. I wasn't hung up on Nick. Nick is one of life's little lessons that I wanted to make sure I never forgot. Apparently I wasn't so successful." She brushed past him through the back door and into the house.

He followed her and made a grab for her arm. "Jo, wait."

She shook him off with an angry jerk of her elbow. "Leave me alone. I don't want to talk to you right now." She kicked the cat kibble out of her way, marched through the kitchen and up the stairs.

Alex rubbed his face with his hands. What was wrong with her? Why couldn't she see what she meant to him? He lowered his hands and spotted the abandoned bag of cat food. The cat had been a mistake. He could see that now.

Once she calmed down, he'd tell her everything.

Chapter Ten

Jo fanned her face with a yellow notepad. Why did the air conditioning always break down on the first really hot day? Even with the door open, the air in Fran's office was stifling. She'd bet the air conditioning in the studio was working perfectly. Alex wouldn't be suffering from the heat.

Alex. Why did her mind keep circling back to him? Ever since that awful scene yesterday, her thoughts had gone around and around with no resolution.

"Mission control to Astronaut Barnett," Ed said loudly. "Do you read me?"

Jo looked at Ed. Clearly she'd missed something he'd said. She'd better try to pay attention.

"Are you feeling all right?" Fran asked.

Jo shifted her gaze to Fran's worried face. "Sure, I'm fine," Jo replied quickly. "Why?"

Fran and Ed exchanged a glance then looked back at Jo.

"Why?" Ed asked, his eyes wide in mock amazement. "Because I've just asked you three times how you think we should kill Tracy off if she decides not to renew her contract next month."

"Tracy's contract is up next month?" Jo asked. It was news to her.

"Have you been having an out-of-body experience and forgot to tell us goodbye? We, that is, Fran and I, have been discussing this for the past fifteen minutes."

Fran aimed a gentle frown in Ed's direction. "Calm down, Ed. Something's on Jo's mind." She turned to Jo. "What's the matter? Tell us. Maybe we can help."

"Nothing's the matter," Jo protested. It sounded weak to her own ears.

"You have to admit you're being unusually quiet," Fran said.

Ed snorted. "Comatose is more like it. Look at her. I can say anything and she doesn't have a single comeback."

Jo ignored Ed and gazed steadily at Fran. It would be a relief to talk to someone who understood how she felt. But where to begin?

"Does it have something to do with Alex?" Fran coached her.

Jo nodded.

Ed tossed his notepad onto the desk. "Okay. Out with it. Tell us everything. I can see we're not going to get any work done until you do."

Maybe she should tell them. They might give her some perspective. "He didn't really need a roommate," she said slowly. "He got the idea when I was evicted. And I kept feeding his cat, but he never had a cat. He made the whole thing up. He says he cares about me, but I just don't know if I can trust him. You can figure why."

Ed shook his head and turned to Fran. "Tragic. One of the finest storytelling minds of our generation, gone. Turned to mush."

Jo sighed. Why was it so hard to explain?

"What are you talking about?" Fran asked Ed. "I understood everything she said. Alex lied and said he needed a roommate to feed his cat to get Jo to move in with him. And we know how Jo feels about being lied to. Remember Nick?"

Jo nodded. Good old Fran, she understood.

"Not the same thing," Ed protested. "Alex must be pretty far gone on Jo to make up a story like that. You'd think she'd be flattered."

"There's nothing flattering about being manipulated, no matter what his motives are," Fran said.

"Okay, I'll buy that," Ed said. "But what I can't figure out is—did Alex eat all that cat food himself?"

"I'm pretty sure it was a possum," Jo replied.

"That does it," Ed said, slapping his hands down on the armrests of his chair. "Call the paramedics. This woman's sense of humor is flat-lining."

"Alex got him from central casting," Jo said quickly. "He was only playing possum."

"Cancel the paramedics," Fran said. "We've got a pulse."

Ed looked at Jo with narrowed eyes. "We may have resuscitated her for now, but what about the next time? We need to do some preventive medicine here."

"I agree with Ed," Fran said. "I take it you two had an argument about this?"

Jo sank a little lower in her chair. "Sort of. I did most of the arguing."

"And now?" Fran asked. "Are you speaking?"

"I don't know. Last night I stayed in my room. He was gone this morning when I got up. I think he had an early call. But he left me a note." She dug in her pocket and pulled out the folded paper, somewhat worn now from having been pulled out of her pocket and read umpteen times since breakfast.

"Too personal for us to see?" Ed asked.

She kept the paper folded over. "He invited me to go with him to the show's anniversary party this Saturday."

"Sounds like a reasonable offer," Ed said.

"He sort of wants to go back to the beginning. He asked me to go with him the first day I met him, and I turned him down." She'd been pretty rude about it, too.

"What about you? What do you want?" Fran asked.

Jo shoved the note back into her pocket. "I don't know. I like him so much, but..."

"It was 'more than like' the last time we discussed the matter," Ed put in. "No real choice here, you know. You have to go. Give the guy a chance to show you he's sincere."

Jo readjusted her seat belt over the the folds of her new dress. She shouldn't have spent so much of her returned rent money on it. Silly, really, to waste money on clothes so she could fix herself up to look like someone she wasn't.

She peered at Alex out of the corner of her eye. He seemed to be giving all his concentration to negotiating through the traffic and had spoken only a few words to her the entire drive into the city.

They'd been wary around one another all week. Not that she'd seen that much of him, his new shooting schedule being what it was. Yet when they were together, they couldn't get around to talking about what was really on their minds. Well, on her mind, anyway. But he was so careful in what he said, how he acted, it had to be on his mind, too. They were roommates, nothing more, and pretty formal roommates, at that. She couldn't figure out how to regain the easy openness they'd had before. Strange how her anger at being manipulated didn't change any of the feelings she had for him.

"I really am sorry, you know," Alex said, as if he'd just been walking around in her mind.

Jo turned her gaze to his profile. It was the first time all week he'd sounded like the old Alex and not someone addressing his maiden aunt. "About what happened? I'm sorry, too," she said.

He turned his head briefly and looked at her, then shifted his gaze back to the traffic in front of them. "I'm glad you came with me tonight. I wasn't sure you would."

"Ed said I should give you a chance to prove your sincerity."

"Ed did?" He sounded surprised.

"He thought a willingness to wear a cummerbund and sit through one of Ron's interminable speeches was a true test of sincerity—or insanity. He wasn't sure which."

Alex laughed then, and melted the last bit of reserve between them. "Maybe it's insanity, because I see the men in white coats," he said, and steered the car into the curving driveway in front of the Fair Hills Hotel. The white-coated parking attendant had Jo's door open practically before Alex had come to a full stop. Jo got out of the car and waited for Alex to get his parking stub.

A manageable number of fans had gathered in front of the hotel and stood politely behind a velvet rope, hoping to catch a glimpse of their favorite soap actors. Two blue-uniformed security guards stood chatting with one another near the hotel entrance.

Alex came around the car and joined her on the sidewalk. He smiled at her, really smiled at her, crinkling eyes and everything, and offered his arm. She returned the smile, took his arm, and they walked together toward the chrome-and-glass entrance of the hotel.

"Johnny!" a fan screamed.

"Johnny, over here!" another yelled. Other voices took up the same cry.

"Your fans await you," Jo said.

"What?" Alex asked.

"They mean you. They think of you as Johnny. Give them a wave."

Alex turned toward the crowd and waved. Several over-eager fans shed their gentility and surged forward, trampling the token velvet barrier under their feet. The security guards scrambled to restore order.

"Can we have your autograph?" one teenager asked, holding out a pen and paper. Alex obliged her and then three others behind her. The security guards made sure they rejoined the group behind the rope as soon as they got their autographs.

Alex put his arm around Jo's waist and ushered her through the wide doorway into the hotel. A third security guard directed them down a long corridor. A full-length mirror in an ornately gilt frame hung at the end of the hallway. Their reflections grew gradually larger as they approached, but strangely enough, those two people in the mirror didn't look like anyone she knew. Alex, of course, was dazzlingly handsome in formal wear. But being dazzling was a piece of cake for him.

Their gazes met in the mirror. Alex bent his head toward her ear. "Did I tell you how lovely you look tonight?" he said softly.

"Thanks," she said, offhand.

Alex stopped in his tracks. "You sound like you don't believe me."

"It's the old Cinderella effect. You look like someone else until midnight."

"You don't sound too happy about it."

"I'm wearing a fancy dress and Sandy got me to put my hair in this up-do. But if you're a pumpkin, you're a pumpkin. I'm never comfortable pretending to be what I'm not."

"Is that how you think of yourself? As a pumpkin?" Alex asked.

Jo set her jaw. "I don't think I'm ugly, but I know I'm not beautiful. I'm a realist." She gestured toward her reflection at the end of the hall. "I know what I see when I look in the mirror."

Alex grabbed her by the hand and pulled her closer to the mirror. "How can someone so smart be so dumb?" He stood behind her, put his hands on her shoulders and spoke to her reflection. "That's not the real you. You can't see your real self, because you have to hold still to look in a mirror."

What was he talking about?

"You could have shaved your head and worn a paper bag tonight, and you'd still be the most fascinating woman in the place." He dropped his hands from her shoulders.

She slowly turned and faced him.

"You don't get it, do you?" Alex went on. "You have a quality I can't describe. You radiate an energy that everyone around can feel. Even when you're sitting still, you're on the move."

No one had ever said anything like this to her before. The casual flattery, the easy comment had frequently come her way, and she'd always brushed them off. But she could feel the intensity vibrating in Alex like her piano's sounding board. He meant every word.

"Are you listening to me?" he asked.

Jo nodded, happiness blossoming in her. "Yes. You said that I was fascinating, that I should've worn a paper bag and borrowed your razor to fix my hair," she replied. "Right?"

"You forgot maddening."

"Did you *say* maddening?"

"I should have."

They stood motionless, gazing at one another. If he didn't take her in his arms in the next second, she was going to throw herself right at him.

"What are you two doing out here in the hall?"

Jo jumped and turned her head.

Tracy, resplendent in a red strapless number, clung to the arm of a handsome blond man. "The party's in there," Tracy said with a toss of her blond mane.

"Hi, Tracy," Alex said.

"This is Cliff," Tracy announced with a wave toward her escort. "Alex and I play opposite one another on 'Triumph,'" Tracy explained to Cliff. "And Jo writes all that great dialogue."

"Nice to meet you, Cliff," Alex said, shaking hands. He stepped back and put an arm around Jo's waist. "You go on ahead. We'll be along in a minute."

Tracy raised her eyebrows, but said nothing. She pulled Cliff toward the ballroom. They disappeared around the corner at the end of the hallway. At the opposite end of the corridor, several more couples approached.

Alex took Jo's hand and led her into an alcove lined with phone booths. She went willingly. She'd do anything to be alone with him, even only semiprivately next to a pay phone.

"I have a little problem," he said, looking down at their linked hands. "I hope you'll help me."

She swallowed hard. "Sure, what is it?" She had a problem herself right now, with her breathing all funny and her heart rate shifting up into high gear.

He raised his gaze from their hands to look at her directly. "Here we are on our first real date, and I'm pretty nervous."

Nervous? What did he know about nervous? She was the one trembling from head to toe. "I make you nervous?" she asked.

He leaned closer to her. The material of his coat brushed her arm. She could smell the spicy fragrance of his shaving soap. "No. I'm nervous because I'm not sure if I'm going to get kissed when the evening ends. Some people don't believe in kissing on a first date."

Jo would have laughed if she'd had enough breath. "You're kidding, right?"

His eyes darkened to a midnight blue. He shook his head solemnly. "No. I'm very serious."

"You want to know if I kiss on a first date?" The words came out in little gasps.

"No." He raised her hand to his face and pressed her palm against his cheek. "I want you to kiss me. Now. Then I won't be nervous all evening just wondering."

"Me?" She couldn't manage full sentences any longer. "Kiss you?"

"Please," he whispered.

She lifted her other hand to his face and pulled him the remaining inches toward her. Her lips trembled slightly at the first contact with his. She pressed them softly, longingly to his. Then she pulled back until she could focus on his face.

"Was that all right?" she breathed.

"I'm still a little nervous. May I have another?" He lowered his face toward her. She kissed him again, gently, and longer this time, moving her mouth against his. She pulled back to break contact, but he moved with her and kept his mouth against hers. She held still, waiting to see what he would do.

"You know what happens now?" he said, breathing the words against her lips.

"What?"

"Now I give you two kisses, so you'll know how much I liked yours." He encircled her with his arms and pulled her body against his.

He kissed her as tenderly as she had kissed him, his mouth answering every movement of hers. She lowered her hands to his chest and leaned against the length of him. He clasped her even tighter, and he became the leader and she the follower. Tenderness gave way to passion and the heat built between them until it threatened to burst into flames.

Alex lifted his head, but still held her tightly. Jo looked up at him, dazed and breathless.

"Was that two kisses already?" she gasped.

"I forgot to keep count." He sounded as out of breath as she. "You know, we still have to go to the banquet." He loosened his hold and moved back a step, but kept her in the circle of his arms.

She leaned toward him, offering herself to him again, her lips parted.

"Jo," he breathed huskily and pulled her close once more. No slow building of heat this time, but an immediate flare of spontaneous combustion, lips and tongues touching, tasting, hands caressing, stroking, and bodies pressed close in a mutual offering of softness and hardness. Jo lost herself in the fire.

Alex dragged his mouth from hers and buried his face in the crook of her neck. "I've waited so long for this," he said, his lips pressed against her bare skin. His warm breath set her awash in heat. She moved her hands restlessly over the hard muscles of his back.

He moved his hands to her shoulders, gripped them tight and pulled himself away from her. "I don't want to, but I think we'd better stop while we still can."

Jo gazed up at him. His face was flushed and his chest heaved with every breath. It was a good thing he still held her away from him, or she would have thrown herself against him again.

He closed his eyes. "Don't look at me like that." He opened his eyes and gazed at her for a long moment. "I take it back. Keep looking at me like that. Don't stop, ever. Come on, let's get this party over with. Then we can go home."

They walked hand in hand out of the alcove. She'd heard the promise in his words. She could wait.

Jo stood just inside the ballroom door clutching Alex's arm. The noise nearly overpowered her bemused brain. Crystal chandeliers sent sparkling light down on the several hundred people gathered for the anniversary banquet. A small band played lively music, but instead of dancing, the guests stood around in their finery talking at the top of their lungs and eyeing all the other guests.

Fran emerged from a tight throng of people and pounced on Jo and Alex. "There you are," she said. Jo could just make out the words over the din of voices. "Where have you been?"

"Alex had to sign autographs for his adoring fans," Jo said, slanting a glance at Alex, daring him to mention what else they'd been doing. The look he flashed back at her made her knees wobbly.

"That lineup of fans is really something. Come on, Ed's over here."

Fran forged a path through the crush of people and Jo followed in her wake with Alex at her elbow, his light touch on her arm a constant reminder of what had just happened between them.

Ed stood to one side of the dance floor, fiddling with a cufflink. "Good, you found them."

"Doesn't Jo look beautiful?" Fran asked. "That dress! And your hair, I've never seen it up like that. It's fantastic."

"That was Sandy's idea," Jo said, slipping her hand into Alex's and leaning slightly toward him. He was anchor, home base, and reality check all in one. Nothing else in the room seemed quite real.

"Ditto to what Fran said," Ed put in.

Fran moved toward her. "How did you do that with your hair?" she asked.

"It's just a clip," Jo explained and released Alex's hand to show her.

Fran stepped closer. "I see," Fran murmured. "I also see that something momentous has taken place here."

"What are you talking about?" Jo asked, her eyes on Alex, who was standing next to Ed, obviously trying to catch what Ed was saying.

"I'm talking about holding hands and doing a great imitation of a thousand-watt bulb. So I take it you two worked things out?"

"I guess so. I mean, yes." Her eyes kept drifting back to Alex. He looked over at her and gave her a little wink.

Linda suddenly appeared in front of her, completely blocking her view of Alex. She wore a vibrantly red strapless dress that looked familiar somehow. Not an altogether flattering style on someone who dieted obsessively to keep herself five pounds underweight.

"You look very nice tonight, Jo," Linda said. "New hairdo, fabulous dress. Necessary, I suppose. Alex is probably a little harder to hang on to than he was to snag in the first place."

"I know this will come as a surprise to you," Jo replied. "But not all women look at relationships from the sport-fishing point of view. I don't expect to 'snag' any man."

The band downshifted from a fast-paced song into a slow number. A few couples glided onto the dance floor, and the general din subsided a little.

"You know, Linda," Fran observed, "I think that dress looks every bit as good on you as it does on Tracy."

"What!" Linda screeched.

So that's where she'd seen it before, Jo scanned the room and easily spotted Tracy in the same red gown. Tracy's figure was as exuberant as the rest of her, and she did the dress justice in a way the gaunt Linda never could.

Alex stepped around Linda and held out his hand to Jo. "I think they're playing our song."

She took his hand and walked onto the dance floor with him. "Do we have a song?" she asked.

"We do now," he said, pulling her close and moving into the rhythm of the music. "Because no matter when or where I hear this song again, I'll always remember tonight, and dancing with you." He pulled slightly away and looked down into her eyes. "Our first dance, with more firsts ahead. Right?"

She melted toward him. "Right," she whispered.

He whirled her around and around and ended in a dip. She dropped her head back, laughing breathlessly, and looked up at the crystal chandelier casting its prisms of light over them like a magic spell of happiness.

Alex helped Jo out of the car and held her hand tightly as they walked along the path to the front door. She'd been waiting for this moment all evening. Through the long, boring, self-congratulatory speeches. Through the dinner, though she couldn't exactly remember eating anything. Through the conversations with all their friends and co-workers. Even through all the dances when they were in each other's arms, close, but never close enough.

He unlocked the door one-handed, guided her inside and shut it firmly behind them. Only then did he release her hand and pull her into his arms. She had her own arms ready and slipped them under his coat to feel the warmth and strength of him through the thin material of his shirt.

Then his mouth took hers, and she was ready for that, too. Her lips parted, offering and demanding at the same time. His hands stroked and caressed her shoulders, waist, hips. She pressed closer to him.

The phone rang.

Jo stilled instantly.

Alex moved his mouth across her cheek to her neck. "Let it go onto the answering machine," he said, his breath hot against her neck. "It's probably a wrong number, anyway."

He did something interesting to her earlobe—something very interesting—and she shivered with delight. But she still listened for a voice to speak through the machine in the kitchen. What was wrong with her? Just a stupid phone call. But what if something had happened to her mother, or Shelley?

"Mr. MacHail, this is Eunice Weeks again."

Alex straightened suddenly, his body tense and listening, his hands still now, but gripping her waist.

Eunice Weeks's voice continued on. "I apologize for leaving so many messages in a row, but the situation seems to change every minute."

"Jo, I'm sorry, but I have to get this call," he said and left her side, striding into the kitchen, flipping on the light as he passed through the doorway.

"The ambassador's cousin will apparently be escorting Buddy on the plane...."

"Mrs. Weeks? Alex here. I just got in."

Jo could hear Alex clearly, though she couldn't see him from where she stood. For some reason her legs weren't feeling too steady. She crossed the hall, got as far as the stairway and sank onto the bottom step. Eunice Weeks had called before and left a message. And Alex had left her that same abrupt way when she'd given him that message.

"Tomorrow? I can't believe it," Alex said into the phone. "It's incredible. Here I was, thinking it'd be months."

Not bad news, anyway. Nobody sick, or hurt, or worse. But they were talking about something important, that much she could tell. Something important to Alex that she didn't know anything about, because Alex was obviously still keeping secrets.

Alex's voice continued more quietly, and she couldn't make out the words. She hugged herself and rested her forehead against her knees. She had a bad feeling about this. A very bad feeling.

"Jo?"

The hall light came on. She raised her head and sat up straight.

"There you are." Alex sat next to her on the stairs and draped his arm around her shoulders. "I have so much to tell you, I don't know where to begin." He squeezed her arm and shifted around as if too excited to sit still.

"I won't say begin at the beginning. I'd rather you went straight to the bottom line."

"The bottom line is that I have a son—an adopted son." He paused and looked at her closely.

"An adopted son..." she echoed. Not an old girlfriend after all, but a child.

"He's not legally mine yet, but it won't be long now. He's an orphan I met when I was in the hospital in Mexico City. We just—connected. Like you and me, you know?"

She stood and moved away from him. She needed room to take this in. Had they "just connected"? That wasn't how she remembered it.

"The red tape and the requirements you have to meet in these kinds of adoptions can drag on forever. But I had a lucky break. The social worker at the adoption agency—"

"Eunice Weeks?" Jo interrupted.

He nodded. "Mrs. Weeks has a friend who knows someone who works at the Mexican consulate here in L.A.," he said, talking fast. "So the friend in the consulate told the wife of the ambassador, and she got all fired up about it and not only cut through all the red tape, but is having her cousin fly in with Buddy tomorrow. Tomorrow—I can't believe it."

She'd never heard him so exuberant before. Maybe if she knew more, it would seem more real. "Buddy, that's not a very Spanish-sounding name. How old is he?"

"He's four. Buddy's a nickname. Actually, his name's Alejandro." He paused a moment. "The same as me—Alexander."

He'd expected her to pick up on the name, even expected her to be excited after he'd blindsided her. She crossed her arms. "I see. So when is Alex Junior arriving?"

"In the morning, ten o'clock. Look, I realize it's kind of a shock, and the timing could be better, but I know you'll love him as much as I do."

"Tell me one thing, Alex. What would be better timing?"

"I wanted to have this night, just for us, without complications. I didn't want to spring Buddy on you like this. Not before, before..."

"We slept together?"

He stood. "No—before I told you I love you."

One bombshell after another. Alex loved her, so he said. She wanted to believe it so much her stomach hurt. "Did you just find this out? Or have you known for a while?"

"That I love you? I told you before, I fell for you the first time I met you. But I don't think I really knew it for sure until I came back from visiting Buddy this last time."

Amazing, he could just drop these explosive devices without blinking an eye. "That was your so-called business trip?"

"You're mad, aren't you?"

Heaven knew she wanted to be mad. How could she have fallen for a man who could keep something this important from her? And what kind of love could he feel for her, when he couldn't even confide in her until he was forced to?

"I'm confused, Alex. I don't know what you want."

He stepped close to her and encircled her with his arms. "I want you, here with me always. I'm serious, Jo. Please don't pull away. You care about me. I know you do."

She held herself stiffly. "You mean a long-term commitment, then."

"A permanent commitment. I want you to marry me."

"You're kidding."

"Name the time and place and see how much I'm kidding."

"I don't want to marry someone who can't trust me."

"What are you talking about? I just told you I love you. I'm asking you to marry me. Doesn't that show trust?"

She pulled free of his arms and paced the width of the hall. "You didn't trust me enough to like you without tricking me into moving in with you. You didn't trust me enough to tell me you were planning on becoming a father. You didn't trust me enough to ask how I'd like being a mother to someone I've never met."

She halted in front of him and put her hands on her hips. "And it just now occurs to me that you didn't trust me enough to tell me the truth about the furniture in your garage. It's for Buddy, isn't it?"

Alex nodded.

"So where's he going to sleep? Maybe you were planning on my room, but you just forgot to mention it?" She should bite her tongue. Everything she said came out crabby, and it wasn't getting them anywhere except farther apart.

"No, I'll move my exercise equipment into my room, and I can fix that room up for him." He rubbed the back of his neck. "You like kids, don't you?" he asked, worry lines forming creases between his brows.

"What's not to like? You forget, I helped raise my sister. That's why I know how hard it can be. I'm not sure you realize what it's like twenty-four hours a day."

"Easy or hard, it's what I want. I thought—I hoped—you'd want it, too."

She let her hands drop to her sides. She couldn't say the words he wanted to hear. She wanted Alex so much she could barely stand to think of it, but not this way, not with so many lies and omissions. Right now she couldn't tell true from false.

"All I know is that I need time to sort things out," she said. "I do care about you, Alex, but everything you've told me—it's all just out of the blue."

He took her hands and she let him pull her close, but when he bent to kiss her, she turned her head. "Please don't. I can't think at all when you kiss me."

"And I can't think of anything else but kissing you."

Sweet talk—he was so good at it. But straight talk, that was another thing. If she let him kiss her, if she went up those stairs and to bed with him the way her body wanted her to, she'd be lost. He'd be able to talk her into anything, whether he really loved her or not.

"I want to wait," she said.

He held on to her hands for a long moment, then released them with a sigh. "All right, we'll wait."

Disappointment swirled around her like a thick fog, chilling the air and dimming the lights. She shifted her weight from foot to foot. She couldn't leave it like this—as if they'd broken up before they'd even gotten together. If he really cared for her, they could work things out between them, given a little time, and a little trust.

"I'll help you get the room ready, if you'd like," she said.

"That's okay. It's late and you should get some sleep. You can help with the finishing touches in the morning."

Get some sleep? He was back to talking to her like his maiden aunt. There didn't seem to be a middle ground for them—at least, not right now. She moved away from him and crossed past him to the stairs. Maybe when she had some time to herself, she'd see things more clearly. Maybe then it wouldn't hurt so much that the magic of the evening had vanished in a puff of smoke. She ran the rest of the way up the stairs.

Chapter Eleven

Jo unlocked the front door and held it open for Alex to carry Buddy inside. Buddy had clung like a limpet to Alex's neck ever since they'd met him at the airport. Not that she could blame him. The noise and chaos there had been enough to make her want to hide. Whose idea had it been to call the media, anyway?

"This is our house," Alex said, pausing at the threshold of the living room.

Buddy lifted his head from Alex's shoulder and peeked back at Jo standing behind them. No wonder Alex had fallen for him. With those enormous brown eyes and tousled black hair he set new precedents for cuteness.

Buddy whispered something in Alex's ear.

Alex turned and faced her. "Jo lives here. She's my friend." He said it as a statement, but his expression turned it into a question.

She gave him look for look. What was this all about? Of course she was his friend—but was that all he wanted from her, friendship? What about last night? The tension between them tautened as if an invisible hand had turned a crank several revolutions.

"How would you like to see your room?" Alex asked with the sudden enthusiasm grown-ups used when they wanted to distract a child.

Buddy smiled and nodded.

Alex lowered him to the floor and took his hand. "Come on. I'll show you."

Jo stood aside and let them go past her to the stairs. Alex held Buddy's small hand in his large one and watched Buddy's every step upward. It was strange to see Alex so tender and gently fussy with this child, so perfectly natural, as if he'd cared for him every day of his life. Why in the world hadn't he told her about Buddy? She still knew next to nothing about him or why Alex had decided to adopt him.

Buddy turned at the landing and looked back. "Jo see my room?"

It was nearly impossible for her to resist that piping little voice, but Alex might like to show Buddy his room by himself. He hadn't wanted her help last night, and this morning he'd let her do very little. "I've seen it, Buddy. You go ahead. I'll be up soon."

She turned and headed for the kitchen, not that she had anything to do in there. Alex had called his catering friend, and he'd delivered a ton of food before they'd left for the airport.

She crossed to the kitchen window and looked out. Buddy's squeals of delight carried all the way downstairs. Not surprising, since Alex had stocked his room with an entire store's worth of toys. He'd nixed her suggestion to save half of them for a later day. And he'd been pretty short with her about it, too, as if she'd implied some criticism.

"Jo?" Alex said from the kitchen doorway.

She turned to face him. He crossed to the island that divided the kitchen from the dining room and rested his hands, palms down, on the counter. If she let herself touch him she'd either hug him or shake him. She'd spent most of the night thinking about him, about them, and got no further than where she was this moment, standing in the kitchen, looking at the man she loved and not knowing if he truly loved her back.

She should bring it up, find some way to break through the constraint between them. "How's it going?" she asked instead.

"Fine. Great. Buddy's playing." He cleared his throat. "So what do you think?" He tapped his fingers on the counter.

It wasn't like Alex to do twitchy things like tapping his fingers. "About Buddy?" She mimed holding up a scorecard. "A definite ten in the Olympic Adorable competition."

He broke into a wide grin. "He is pretty cute, isn't he?"

"Speaks English well, too."

"I had him tutored, but I don't want him to lose his Spanish. That's part of his heritage. I found an agency with bilingual baby-sitters. I guess I should put in a call. Do you think anyone would be there on a Sunday?" He moved toward the phone.

"You're going to get a baby-sitter for him?" Jo asked.

Alex paused on his way to the phone. "Of course. I still have to work."

"I meant, since he's four, I thought you'd put him in nursery school."

"No, I want him at home. He's been in an institution all his life."

"All the more reason. He's already used to a fairly structured day. Besides, he might get really bored without other kids to play with."

"The sitter will play with him and take care of him. He won't get in your way."

"What a thing to say. I was thinking of what might be best for Buddy."

He rubbed the back of his neck. "Sorry. I'm a little tired. I didn't think."

She couldn't take this anymore. She had to say what was on her mind. "We have to talk."

"I recognize that line. What did you tell me—now we cut to a three-second reaction shot of your face?"

Humor, always a good sign. If they could laugh, they could work this out. "You're right. I've been reading too much of my own dialogue. I…" She didn't know how to get this out. She had to ask, but was so scared what the answer might be.

He came around the counter and put his hands on her shoulders. "Go ahead. Tell me off. I know I haven't handled any of this very well."

"That's not it. I have to ask you. Just tell me the truth—please."

"Jo, I know it's going to be hard for you to believe, but I don't ordinarily lie."

"I have to know about Buddy's adoption. Don't you need to be married to do that?"

He tightened his grip on her shoulders. "No. I'm adopting as a single parent. That's one of the reasons it took so long. You think that's why I proposed?"

It did sound silly when she said it out loud, here in the sun-filled kitchen with Alex's hands warm on her shoulders and his gaze even warmer on her face. She wrinkled her nose at him.

He bent and kissed her nose. "You are the most mistrustful person I've ever met."

"*Papi,*" Buddy called from upstairs. "Come play."

"Be right there," Alex called back.

"Jo come, too," Buddy said.

It sounded like an order. Alex raised a questioning eyebrow.

"Yes, Jo come, too," she said.

Alex gave her shoulders a squeeze and dropped a kiss lightly on her lips.

She responded by giving him a playful peck back. There wasn't time now for more, but it didn't matter. Everything would work out fine for them now.

* * *

Jo parked her car neatly in the garage, shut off the engine and hopped out. There was no car on Alex's side of the garage. A little pinprick of disappointment jabbed at her. She really shouldn't be surprised. The cast was shooting later and later these days. But the past week hadn't gone quite as she'd expected, and she had an increasing hunger to be around him, a longing for their old friendly intimacy.

She walked out of the garage and fit her key into the outside panel. The garage door rattled down. If only she could find a way to break through the strange constraint Alex wore like a shield when he was around her. He was affectionate to her, but that's as far as it went. Sometimes she'd catch him looking at her with some of that old high-voltage electricity in his gaze, and she'd get all quivery inside. But he never tried to kiss her breath away.

The garage door clunked to a halt. She pulled her key out, dropped it in her purse, then headed up the flagstones to the front door. Coming home to Buddy was a whole new experience. After only one week of instant, unofficial parenthood, she'd fallen under the spell of that brown-eyed, black-haired bundle of energy.

She slipped in the front door and closed it behind her. "Hi," she called. "Anybody home?"

An answering high-pitched shout came from the kitchen followed by the sound of running feet. Buddy raced into the front hall, arms outspread, but he stumbled before he could reach her. Jo dived toward him and caught him up in her arms.

"Oh, my gosh, you're so heavy." She hoisted him up and pretended to stagger under his weight. "What did you do? Gain ten pounds today?"

Buddy laughed and wriggled in her arms. She set him down carefully, making sure his feet were securely under him before she let go. He fell a lot when he ran, more than he should, really. Had Alex noticed it? Maybe she should mention it to him.

"What're you up to, big boy?" she asked him.

"I'm hungry, and Carmelina won't give me nuffing to eat," he complained.

"Buddy, that is not true," Carmelina called from the kitchen. She had the nicest voice—like singing bells, and she'd turned out to be just as nice as her voice. Alex had been really lucky to find such a good baby-sitter right off the bat.

Jo looked down at Buddy. "Starving you, huh? Why do I find that hard to believe?"

Buddy tugged at her hand and led her into the kitchen.

"Hi, Carmelina. How did it go today?" Jo asked.

Carmelina looked up from the counter where several plates of food rested among opened cans and refrigerator containers. "I tried to give him some dinner." She gestured toward the plates and containers. "But he wouldn't eat anything he asked for."

"He wouldn't, huh?" Jo raised an eyebrow at Buddy, then turned back to Carmelina. "Everything okay otherwise?"

"Yes, just fine. He's got a lot of energy, you know?"

"Yes, I've noticed that," Jo said. She turned to Buddy. "All right, it looks like you have three choices here." She pointed to the plates on the counter. "Which one do you want?"

"I don't like them."

"Didn't Carmelina give you what you asked for?"

Buddy stuck out his lower lip in a rebellious pout. "I don't like them," he said again.

"This is the deal," Jo said matter-of-factly. "You can eat one of the dinners Carmelina's fixed for you now, or you can wait till you're really hungry and eat one of them later."

"I don't like them," Buddy yelled.

"When you sign your first five-million-dollar record deal," Jo said, "you can send as many dinners back to the kitchen as you want. Until then—if you ordered it, you eat it."

"I don't like you," Buddy announced, his eyes snapping with anger.

What a time-warp sensation that gave her. Shelley used to say the same thing when she didn't get her way. "That's all right. I like you."

Buddy whirled around and stomped out of the room. Jo lifted her gaze to meet Carmelina's. "Is he like that with you?" Jo asked.

"He's very good. He never talks back or anything," Carmelina said.

"But you fixed him three different dinners."

Carmelina shrugged. "Alex said to give him whatever he wanted to eat."

Jo dropped her gaze. Alex wouldn't say no to Buddy. About anything. She'd have to face up to that reality pretty soon, because it certainly affected their life together—what life together they had.

"You want me to watch Buddy now, so you can get on home?" Jo asked.

"That's all right. I'll wait for Alex." Carmelina got very busy cleaning up all the food on the counter.

"Guess I'll take a swim, then," Jo said, trying to sound offhand. She headed upstairs to her room. Strange, the way Carmelina had acted. She closed the door to her room and quickly shucked out of her clothes and into her swimsuit. Had Alex told Carmelina not to leave Buddy in her care? She stopped in midmotion. There, she'd gone and let that bad thought in, that niggling notion in the back of her mind—Alex didn't want her involved in caring for Buddy.

She grabbed her towel and hurried downstairs. Buddy sat on the bottom step, with his chin propped in his hands. Shelley used to sit just like that after she'd had a snit. In fact, Buddy reminded her a lot of Shelley.

Jo stepped around Buddy and crouched down facing him. "How're you doing?"

"Not so good."

Jo waited for him to get it off his chest.

His lower lip quivered. "I yell and say bad things to you, and you mad at me."

"I'm not mad at you. You know why? I have a little sister, and when she was your age, she'd want her way, just like you. And she'd yell and get mad, just like you. And I figured out that I didn't have to get mad back." No point in telling him it had taken her about eight years to learn that lesson.

"I'm sorry."

"I can see that. How about a hug?" She held out her arms and Buddy slipped off the step into her embrace. "I'm going for a swim. Would you like to go swimming with me?"

He shook his head. "I don't like it."

"Okay, see you in a little bit." She straightened and crossed to the kitchen and out the back door.

She'd asked him before to go to the pool with her. He always refused, saying he didn't like the water. She'd wanted to start a water safety program with Buddy right away, but Alex had insisted she wait until Buddy wanted to. That was just one more thing they needed to talk about.

She passed through the back gate and pulled it shut behind her until she heard the latch click. The towel went on its usual chair, then two steps and she stood at the pool's rim. She hit the water in a straight-to-the-bottom dive, submerging herself in the familiar shock of cool water. Swimming was the best way in the world for her to stop thinking—about Alex not talking to her, about Alex not trusting her, about Alex not kissing her anymore.

She surfaced and stroked to the end of the pool, flip-turned and stroked to the other end. She gave herself over to the repeated motions of her arms and legs and her rhythmic breathing with every other stroke. Stroke, stroke, breathe. Let the water become the entire universe. Stroke, stroke, breathe. Let everything else float away. Stroke, stroke...

"Jo!" Buddy called.

She choked on some water, recovered and turned over on her back to see where his voice had come from. Buddy was running pell-mell toward the pool.

"Buddy! No running!" she cried.

He didn't listen, or maybe he couldn't hear her. She side-stroked rapidly toward the rim of the pool. Buddy hurtled on, his legs pumping. He came to a near stop right at the pool's edge, but tripped at the last second and toppled into the pool without a sound, except the small splash his body made as it hit the water.

She swam toward the spot where he'd gone down. It had never taken her this long to swim a length. *Stay calm. Stay calm. You'll get to him.*

Afraid of the water, he was afraid of the water, and he hadn't come up yet. *Come on, Buddy, surface.* She sucked in a lungful of air and dived.

Buddy hung suspended in the blue water, arms and legs flailing. She came up under him, grabbed him by the waist and pushed his head above the surface. He became strangely lighter the higher she pushed him out of the water, until he defied gravity completely and floated out of the pool.

She surfaced and looked up. Alex stood on the cement ledge, a wailing Buddy wrapped in his arms.

"What the hell do you think you're doing?" he shouted at her.

She flipped her wet hair away from her face. "Don't you swear at me, Alex MacHail," she shouted back over Buddy's continued wails. "I didn't do anything except have the scare of my life."

One small kick took her to the pool's edge. With a push of her arms she hoisted herself out and onto her feet. Her knees could have been steadier, but she'd be darned if she'd let Alex see that.

She marched over to her towel and brought it back to where Alex stood holding Buddy. "Here, Buddy, let's wrap you up and take you inside. You got all wet, didn't you?"

Buddy stopped his crying on a hiccup and buried his face against Alex's shoulder. Jo wrapped him as best she could with Alex lifting first one arm, then the other. Her hands shook visibly as she tucked the towel around Buddy. She couldn't look at Alex.

"Do you think I deliberately let Buddy run around the pool while I took my swim?" she asked, her voice shaking as much as her hands. "He was with Carmelina. I closed the gate all the way. I'm sure of it. The latch is on this side. I don't know how he got through."

Buddy shifted his head so he could see her. "I climb up, and I can reach. *Papi* and Carmelina were talking. I wanted to watch you swim."

"So what are you going to do now?" she said to Alex. "Go in and yell at Carmelina? If you'd let me teach him basic water safety, this might not have happened."

"Jo," Alex said quietly. "I'm sorry I yelled at you. I was just so scared, I didn't think."

"*You* were scared? What about me? I'm afraid to look in the mirror. My hair's probably turned white." Joking had always been her best defense, but why should she have to defend herself against Alex?

Buddy lifted his head from Alex's shoulder and stared at her, wide-eyed. "Your hair is not white, Jo," he said.

"Thank goodness for that, but it is wet—and so are you. And look at Alex. He's wet, too, and he didn't even get to go swimming. Let's go put on some dry clothes." She made to move away, but Alex put out his free arm and stopped her.

"I owe you a big apology. It's my fault this happened. I should've been paying more attention. I'm so grateful you were here." He pulled her toward him and gave her a one-armed hug.

Now he wanted to hug her and thank her for saving Buddy. She leaned her head against his shoulder, too weak willed to resist whatever affection he chose to show her.

"Buddy," Jo called from the foot of the stairs. "Where are you?" Here she was, in charge of taking care of Buddy for the first time, and she couldn't even find him. Carmelina had been in a tizzy about leaving him, but with her mother ill and Alex on a late night shoot, she had no choice.

Carmelina had acted as if Jo would find it a terrific bother to take care of Buddy. Alex must have told her that, and even though she'd already guessed as much, it still hurt.

She hurried up the stairs. "Buddy," she called again as she neared the top. A giggling Buddy, dressed only in a T-shirt and underpants, with a pillowcase for a cape, dashed down the hall.

"Buddy, want to go out to dinner with me?"

Fran and Ed had invited her to dinner just before Carmelina came to ask her to take care of Buddy. They'd been pretty insistent that she come. Something must be up. Well, she could take Buddy with her. He'd probably really like it. Alex kept him home too much, anyway.

A rhythmic thudding came from Buddy's room. Jo headed hastily toward the sound. Buddy stood in the middle of his bed jumping up and down over and over again, arms stretched above his head. A loud thud followed every jump. "I'm Super Buddy," he shouted. He pushed off again on sturdy legs and—what were those scars on his foot?

Jo strode to the side of his bed. "Super Buddy, wait a minute. No more flying right now." She made a grab for him, but Buddy, who loved tag more than anything, slipped out of her grasp and hopped to the other end of the bed. She moved toward him, faked to her right and caught him when he tried to go left. He squealed with delight as he always did, since, for him, getting caught was as much fun as trying to get away.

Laughing herself, Jo pinned him to the bed, and said, "I just realized I've never seen your bare feet before. It looks like you had an operation."

Buddy stuck his foot out and looked at it. "I had a bad foot. The doctors fixed it."

One more secret Alex had kept from her. He'd given her such a small role in Buddy's care, that she hadn't even seen his foot without shoes and socks or sleeper pajamas. And when she'd mentioned about Buddy's tendency to fall when he ran, Alex had brushed her off.

"Did you have the operation a long time ago?"

"The first 'peration was long, long time ago."

He'd had more than one. Jo's hand closed over Buddy's small foot. "So you probably don't remember that one."

"I always remember. I find *Papi* when I wake up."

"*Papi* was with you when you had your operation?"

"No. I find him—after. He played with me all the time."

"You mean in the hospital?"

Buddy nodded. "We are the same three . . ." He held up three fingers. "Three . . . I don't know what word."

"That's okay. What are the three things?"

He counted on his fingers. "Same name. Same leg. Same . . ." He hesitated and frowned. "*¿Cómo se dice huérfano?*"

"I'm not sure. Orphan?" Did he think Alex was an orphan, too?

"*Sí*, orphan. *Papi* did not have a little boy, and I did not have a *papi*. And I said, 'I be your little boy' and *Papi* said, 'That best offer I got all day!'" Buddy fairly shouted.

The story had the rhythms of a tale lovingly told and retold. So why hadn't Alex ever told her? She looked down at the small foot she still held in her hand and, with her fingertip, traced the pattern of scars that encircled it. If only she could have been there, too, when Buddy woke up, and played with him, and fallen in love with him, at the same time Alex had. It wasn't fair that she should be left out, when she wanted so desperately to belong to this child and his father.

"Why you cry?" Buddy asked.

She blinked to focus her eyes, and gazed down at her hands. She'd covered Buddy's foot with her tears. She bent her head and pressed her lips to one of the angry red lines on his foot. Buddy patted her shoulder.

"Don't cry. It's all better now," he said.

"It is?" Jo swiped at her tears and put on a deliberately devilish expression. "Then maybe I'd better kiss it again." She kissed his foot several times.

Buddy laughed and squirmed free from her grasp. "That tickles." He stood on the bed and jumped up and down again, watching to see what she'd do.

"Buddy, you're jumping again."

"Yes," he said, eyes sparkling with glee. "I'm jumping."

Jo wrestled him to the bed. "Then I guess I'd better... kiss your foot." She smothered his foot with kisses.

Buddy shrieked with laughter, twisted out of her grip and resumed jumping with all the determination of someone intent on repeating the same game for as long as possible. Jo stood poised by the side of the bed, ready to pounce, when the phone rang.

"I should answer that." She moved toward the door. "You stop jumping while I'm out of the room, okay? I don't want you to fly off the bed and crash-land."

Buddy gave a few short bounces, then sat on the bed. Jo rushed across the hall to Alex's room, grabbed up the phone by the side of his bed and gasped out, "Hello."

"Hello. May I please speak to Alex?"

Jo froze for a second. She had some bad associations with that voice. "Is this Mrs. Weeks?" she asked, though she knew darn well it was.

"Yes. And you're Ms. Barnett, aren't you? How are you?"

"Fine." What did she want—to check up on Buddy? "We're all really fine. Very happy."

"I'm not surprised. Well, let me add my own best wishes. Have you set a date yet?"

"A date? You mean for adopting Buddy?"

"No. I meant for your wedding."

Chapter Twelve

Jo's legs wobbled under her. She sat down on the floor, next to the bed, clutching the phone in two hands. "Alex told you we were getting married?"

"It wasn't supposed to be a secret, was it?"

"No, of course not." She had to think fast. Eunice Weeks had some power over this adoption process, though what exactly, she had no idea. "I'm just curious—when did he tell you?"

"That day I phoned. We spoke, remember?"

How could she forget? She'd never been given the third degree over the phone before. "Oh, right," she said with a breathy, phony-sounding laugh. She had to end this call before she lost it completely. "Can I take a message for you?"

"I can tell you just as well. The county social worker will be setting up an appointment with you very soon. You don't want to put off meeting with her, because your court date is based on when she files her report, usually a hundred and eighty days after filing."

"I don't understand. Court date? I thought you were the social worker on Buddy's case."

"My agency helped Alex bring Buddy into the United States, but the State of California requires that adoptive parents be interviewed by a state-employed social worker. The judge looks at her recommendation in deciding whether to approve the adoption or not."

"I see," Jo murmured. What did she see, really? A whole lot of pain and grief lay ahead for her when she finally let everything sink in. "Thanks for calling. I'll let Alex know."

"Why don't you call me after you talk to the social worker? Tell me how the interview went, although I'm certain she'll give you both a very favorable report."

"I'll do that. Bye now."

"Goodbye. Enjoy that sweet little boy."

"Thanks, we will." She held the phone on her lap for a second, then without getting up from the floor, she reached blindly above her head and hung it up. She'd been wrong about Eunice Weeks. She only sounded stuffy.

She'd been wrong about Alex, too. He only sounded sincere. He'd told Eunice Weeks they were going to get married at least a week before he'd asked her to marry him. He'd proposed after he'd heard that Buddy was on his way, and then only because it would help him adopt Buddy.

She pulled her knees up and rested her forehead against them. Alex had lied to her all along. And now that Buddy had captured her own heart, she couldn't say that she blamed him. She might have done the same thing herself, if she thought she had to. What was she going to do now?

"You crying?" Buddy asked.

She lifted her head. Buddy stood in front of her, still in underpants and T-shirt, his pillowcase cape dragging from one hand.

"No. I'm not crying," she said. "I was feeling a little sad, but here you are, and I'm not sad now."

She straightened her legs to make a lap and held out her arms. Buddy sat down and nestled against her as if this was his rightful place. As far as she was concerned, he did belong there, and in her heart, for always. So did Alex.

But Alex had other ideas. He wanted a paper mother for Buddy. If he'd wanted a real mother for him, he would've let her act like a mother, and not kept her on the fringes of his life with Buddy.

Jo backed her car into a spot only two doors down from the restaurant. The god of parking places must have smiled down on her tonight. Thank goodness Buddy had distracted her for the entire drive into the city by firing one question after another at her.

Fran and Ed would provide even more distraction. There they were, waiting for her in front of the restaurant. She got out of the car, waved to them, then helped Buddy with the straps of his car seat. Buddy stared wide-eyed and open-mouthed, taking in the lights and the busy street scene.

"I want up," he said in a little voice.

Jo picked Buddy up and turned to face Fran and Ed who were hurrying over to them.

"We're so glad you could make it," Fran said.

Buddy hid his face against Jo's shoulder.

"I have a surprise," Jo said. "I brought Buddy with me so you can finally meet him."

"Well, where is he?" Ed asked.

Buddy clutched Jo tighter and buried his face even further against her shoulder.

"I brought him with me. Really I did," she said.

"You did?" Ed asked. "I can't see him anywhere."

She felt Buddy stirring in her arms. He'd never be able to resist the challenge of the game. Good old Ed. Who would have thought he'd be good with kids?

"I wonder where could he be?" Fran asked.

"Here I am!" Buddy announced, raising his head from her shoulder and smiling widely at everyone.

Ed clutched at the front of his shirt. "Good Lord, what a scare you gave me. I never even saw you there."

"Hello, Buddy," Fran said. "I'm so happy to meet you. I'm Fran, and the silly one with me is Ed."

"Well, sir," Ed said to Buddy. "I must say it's a great pleasure to make your acquaintance at last."

Buddy giggled and didn't hide his face again.

Silly only partly described Ed. He also looked happy. Could it be that cynical, skeptical, sardonic Ed Selkin had found happiness? She looked back and forth from Ed to Fran. They both radiated an aura of private, glowing bliss.

Jo looked straight at Ed. "You finally told her, didn't you?"

"We couldn't wait to tell you," Fran answered for him. "He finally confessed his feelings, thanks to you and Alex," she added.

"My *papi?*" Buddy piped up.

"Yes, indeed," Ed said. "Your *papi* and Jo looked so enchanted with one another one night not so long ago that they inspired me to declare my undying devotion to my beloved." He scooped up Fran's hand and pressed it to his lips. "So we're going to tie the hitch."

"That's right," Fran said, gazing at Ed adoringly. "We're going to get knotted."

Buddy leaned toward Jo's ear. "They talk funny," he said in a loud whisper.

"What they mean," Jo explained, "is that they love each other, and they're going to get married."

"I can't even begin to tell you how much I've wished for this," she told them. "I'm so happy for you." She meant it, too, with all her heart—except for one small, sad corner of her heart that wished she could have found the same happiness with Alex.

Buddy leaned toward her ear again. "I want us to get marry, too."

"Us? You and me?"

"You and me and *Papi*. All of us get marry and we have *una familia grande.*"

She hugged him, ducking her face away from Fran and Ed, and blinking the sudden tears from her eyes. "I love you so much."

Fran must have heard the catch in her voice. "Are you okay, Jo?"

She straightened and smiled across at them. "I'm fine," she lied. "Just fine."

Alex paced to the living-room windows and stared out into the darkness. Where the hell were Jo and Buddy? He strode back into the kitchen and looked at the notepad by the phone for the twentieth time. She could have left a note, something, anything to let him know what had happened.

He grabbed up the phone, then jammed it back on the hook. Who could he call? He'd already phoned Carmelina, and she didn't know anything, except that Jo had been really happy to take care of Buddy.

If only he could believe it. Granted, it had to have come as a shock that he had a kid, but she'd closed right down. He'd kept Buddy out of her way just to show her raising a kid wasn't that hard.

Who was he kidding? He'd never done anything harder. But Jo wouldn't act like a partner. She disagreed with him at every turn—nursery school, bedtime, meals, swimming lessons. Okay, maybe she'd been right about the swimming lessons.

Swimming...what if he'd fallen in the pool again? Alex pressed a fist against his forehead. The image of Buddy struggling underwater kept popping into his head. He never knew when it would hit him, but every time it did, the same sick terror swamped him. He'd blown a whole scene because of it just the other day.

He had to get a grip on himself. Buddy couldn't have fallen into the pool again. He'd put the lock on the gate himself and had had a long talk with Buddy about it.

Wait—did he hear a key turning in the front-door lock? Three paces took him into the front hall. Jo stepped through the door carrying a sleeping Buddy in her arms.

"Thank God, you're home," Alex said. "Is Buddy all right?"

Jo looked at him, her eyes wide in surprise. "What are you talking about?"

"I come home and no one's here. So naturally I'm kind of worried, and you haven't even left a note."

"Sorry—I forgot to."

She didn't look very sorry. He'd been going crazy for an hour, and she shrugged it off. "Well—what happened?"

"Nothing happened. Buddy and I went out to dinner with Fran and Ed. Guess what? They're—"

"You what! You took Buddy out at night in that crate you call a classic car just so you could eat out? Was it such a strain to stay in one night and take care of him?"

Jo stuck her chin out. "I did take care of him. My car is perfectly safe, and I have an impeccable driving record. Buddy had a wonderful time for once. *You* never take him anywhere."

"You're damn right, I don't take him out at all hours when he should be home asleep, and I sure don't risk him getting pneumonia again by taking him out at night."

"Listen, I'm the one who suggested he have a regular bedtime. You're the one who lets him stay up as late as he wants. And how am I supposed to know anything about him catching pneumonia, when you haven't told me anything about it?" She lifted her chin with a jerk and glared at him.

Alex clenched his jaw and glared back. Maybe he should have told her about Buddy's foot, about the pneumonia he'd had after the last surgery. But then she might have turned away, believing Buddy wasn't normal. No, she didn't understand anything, and it didn't matter that he loved her with everything he had. If she couldn't love Buddy, they couldn't stay together.

"Got you there, didn't I?" she went on. "Well, you don't have to tell me anything now, because I know everything—including the fact that you've been passing me off as your fiancée."

"I don't know what you're talking about."

"Don't bother with the act. Eunice Weeks filled me in. I know that you planned on producing me as future mother for the county social worker's approval."

"Maybe I made a mistake about that. Maybe you're not good mother material after all." The words slipped out somehow.

Jo flinched as if he'd slapped her and stared at him. Her eyes brimmed with tears, but she blinked them back. "Here," she said, her face pale and set, "since you don't trust me to put him to bed, you'd better do it. It's late." She handed Buddy into his arms.

He lifted Buddy, hefting his warm weight until Buddy's head rested against his shoulder.

Buddy stirred and opened his eyes. "Hi, *Papi*. Where's Jo?"

"I'm right here." Jo stepped close to Alex's side where Buddy could see her. "Daddy's going to put you in bed now. It's very late. Good night." She kissed Buddy's cheek and whispered, "I love you" in his ear.

Buddy leaned halfway out of Alex's arms to give Jo a fierce hug around the neck. "I love you, too," he said.

Alex balanced the child in his arms as he shifted his weight back toward him. He peered at her, but she kept her face averted. If she really did love Buddy, maybe they could work things out. "Jo..." he said.

Without looking at him, she held up her hand. "Later, okay?" She turned quickly and ran up the stairs.

He followed slowly with Buddy snuggling sleepily against his neck.

"*Papi?*" Buddy said, his voice muffled against Alex's shoulder. "Can we go to that place again?"

He carried his son into his room and lowered him onto his bed. "The restaurant? Sure."

He'd talk to Jo, find out what she really felt, just as soon as he got Buddy in bed. He unlaced Buddy's shoes, pulled them off, then stripped off his socks. "Did you have fun?"

Buddy blinked drowsily up at the ceiling. "Lots of fun. I like Ed. He's funny."

Alex rifled through Buddy's top dresser drawer. "He's a funny guy, all right." He held up two pairs of pajamas. "What do you want to wear tonight? The cowboys or the baseballs?"

Buddy pointed to the cowboys. Alex dropped the baseball pajamas back into the drawer and pushed it shut. "Okay, let's get you out of those clothes." He crossed back to the bed.

All of a sudden Buddy didn't look sleepy anymore. He rolled away from Alex's grasp and pushed himself to his feet on the bed.

"Buddy, it's late. Time for bed."

Buddy looked at him, his eyes glittering, and jumped up and down on the bed. "I'm jumping," he announced.

He didn't have time for this. He had to talk to Jo. He caught the boy in midjump and sat him on the bed. Buddy immediately stuck his foot up in the air.

"I already got your shoes and socks off. Now it's time for your pants and shirt," Alex said.

"Kiss it," Buddy commanded.

"Kiss your foot? Forget it. Now get out of those clothes."

"Jo kissed my foot."

Alex stopped cold. "Jo did?" He sat next to Buddy on the bed. "When?"

"Today. She cried and got it all wet. She was sad for my foot, but I told her it was all better, and she kissed it and kissed it. And I jumped on the bed and she catched me and kissed my foot again. So you kiss it." He lay back on his pillow and held his foot up in the air.

Alex put his lips on the small, scarred foot, the old lump back in his throat again. What a picture—Jo crying over Buddy's foot, then making a game out of it. That was his Jo, all right. Only maybe she wasn't his Jo anymore. She probably hated him now.

He helped Buddy out of his clothes and into his pajamas. Buddy must have jumped the last bit of energy out of himself, because he slid willingly under the covers.

Alex bent over for one last good-night hug.

"Can we get marry?" Buddy asked. "You and me and Jo?"

Alex stroked his son's cheek. "Would you like that?"

Buddy nodded. "I want us to get marry and have brothers and sisters."

"We'll have to ask Jo about it. See what she says."

"I ask her already."

"What did she say?"

"She say she loves me."

Of course she loved Buddy. Why couldn't he have seen that before? "I love you, too."

That got him another big hug. "Good night, *Papi*."

Alex crossed to the door and turned off the light. "Good night."

He walked down the hall to Jo's room. Her door stood ajar, but the room lay in darkness. "Jo?" he called softly. No answer. Had she gone downstairs to wait for him? He hurried down to the brightly lit kitchen. A note lay on the counter by the phone. He snatched it up.

Dear Alex,
I understand why you did it. I'd have done the same thing, if I were in your shoes. But I know you see now, as clearly as I do, that it can't work if you don't love me. I'll send movers for my things as soon as possible.
Jo

He crumpled the note in his fist and slumped against the counter. She loved him, and she loved Buddy. He didn't deserve her, but he was going to get her back anyway.

Whatever it took.

Chapter Thirteen

Alex knocked on Fran's office door, then opened it without waiting for an invitation. Fran looked up from her desk. "Where's Jo?" he asked.

"Hi, Alex," Fran replied slowly, almost warily. "Have a seat." She waved toward the two other chairs.

Alex sat heavily in the chair Jo always used. "I called you and Ed last night and left messages on your machines. I know you know where she is."

"She doesn't want to talk to you."

He leaned toward her. "Where is she?"

"She's really hurting, Alex. The kindest thing would be to leave her alone."

"I know she's hurt, and it's all my fault. But if I could just see her for a few minutes. Make her understand."

"Understand what?"

"I love her. I can't make it without her. I've been a jerk, but I can make her understand. I know I can."

Fran looked at him a few moments without speaking. "You really do love her, don't you?"

"I've loved her all along, but I messed up by trying to control everything."

Ed walked into Fran's office, unannounced. He stopped abruptly in the doorway, looked at Alex and frowned. "You look terrible. Almost as bad as Jo."

He got to his feet at once and grabbed Ed by the lapels. "Where is she?"

"Hey, take it easy on the imported tweed." Ed pulled his jacket from Alex's grip and patted it flat. "She doesn't want to see you. Anyway, aren't you supposed to be working?"

Alex clenched and unclenched his fists. He needed to calm down. Fran and Ed were Jo's best friends, and if anyone knew how to reach her, they did. "I called in sick."

"You're kidding, right?" Ed said. "Don't you know that actors working for Ron Fisk never call in sick? Fevers of a hundred and four, complete laryngitis, paralysis of the lower limbs—your scenes can be directed around them. Hence, if you call in sick, you must be malingering. He'll have your head."

"I have to see Jo."

Ed looked at Fran. "He sounds determined."

"He loves her," Fran said. "He really loves her."

Ed looked back at Alex with new interest in his eyes. "He loves her? That's a different story altogether." Ed took two steps, bent and placed a kiss directly on Fran's mouth. "That's a language we understand. Right, light of my life?"

Alex stared at them. "What's going on here?"

Ed straightened and announced, "We're engaged. Jo didn't mention it? We had a little celebration dinner last night."

So that was what Jo had tried to tell him. Alex stuck out his hand and shook Ed's. "Congratulations."

He turned to Fran. "And best wishes."

Fran beamed back at him. "Thank you."

"Look, I know you're Jo's friends, and you want to protect her. But I love her, and I want to marry her, so can you help me out?"

"She's down the hall in the conference room," Fran said. "We have a major meeting that starts in about—" she consulted her watch "—three minutes."

She'd been down the hall all the time. Why didn't they say that before? Alex moved to go past Ed and out the door.

"Wait a minute." Ed blocked his way. "You can't see her until after the meeting."

"Why not? I have to talk to her." Why weren't they helping him? Maybe he should grab Ed's coat again. Ed must have thought he was going to, because he took a step backward.

"Three very big reasons." Ed counted on his fingers. "One, top executives from Countrel Enterprises will be there on their semiannual make-life-miserable-for-writers junket. They don't like to have meetings disrupted."

What did he care about company executives? He sidestepped Ed and headed out the door.

Ed came out with him, matching his stride.

"Wait for me," Fran called.

"Two," Ed said. "Ron will have you hanged at dawn for disrupting the meeting."

Once past the elevators and the reception desk, Alex slowed his steps slightly. "Where's the meeting?"

"Last door on the right," Fran said from behind him.

"Fran, you're not helping." Ed skipped ahead of Alex a couple of steps, turned and walked backward in front of him, holding up three fingers. "Three, if you make a scene, you might get Jo fired."

Alex stopped in his tracks.

Fran bumped into him from behind. "Sorry," she said, and moved around him to stand next to Ed.

"Get her fired?" Alex asked. "How do you figure that?"

"Think about it," Ed said. "You know Jo's style. You go in there and say you'd like to have a private word with her, and she'll punch your lights out—verbally, that is."

"Ed's right," Fran agreed. "She's really hurt, completely devastated. She's bound to get mad at you if you try to see her. That's how she is."

"And in that crowded room, someone's going to get caught in the cross fire," Ed said. "Probably Ron, because he won't be able to keep his mouth shut."

"She wouldn't be subtle, either," Fran added. "So Ron would get what she was saying—maybe. And he hates being laughed at."

"Yes, he's funny that way," Ed put in.

Alex shook his head. He had to see Jo. He couldn't wait any longer. He'd already gone through an agonizing eternity last night. He held both hands out toward them. "You're her friends. Help me. I have to see her—now."

Fran and Ed looked at each other, some kind of wordless communication flowing between them.

"Excuse us a moment," Fran said to Alex. "We have to consult." She pulled Ed aside and whispered to him urgently.

Ed nodded several times, listening. Then he rubbed his chin and gazed at Alex. "We might pull it off, if we talk fast enough."

Jo lined up her pen next to her notebook and folded her hands on top of the conference table. Ron sat at the head of the table chatting happily with one of the vice presidents of something or other. Bea and Dorothy did likewise from their places at the other end of the table.

She should make an effort herself and say something to the gray-suited vice president who sat next to her, but lack of sleep had turned her brain to oatmeal. Her heart still hurt just as much, though. She needed a major distraction, like work, lots of hard work. Then, maybe, she could go without thinking about Alex for as long as a minute.

The door opened. Fran and Ed slipped in with Alex right behind. She clenched her folded hands. What was he doing here? She couldn't stay in the same room with him, not now. She couldn't bear it. But somehow she couldn't move. She remained motionless in her chair, as if frozen.

"Ah, here we are," Ron said. "Gentlemen, I believe you remember Fran Marcus and Ed Selkin from our meeting last fall. And here's Alex MacHail, our rising new star." Ron's voice went up an octave. A sure sign of stress. He didn't know why Alex had come to the meeting, either. Somebody had better come up with a good reason, or Ron's blood pressure would be rising as fast as Alex's star would be falling.

She glanced up at Fran and Ed. How could they do this to her? They didn't return her gaze. Ed busily helped Fran into her seat, then sat down himself. Alex took the place opposite Jo, and she turned her head to avoid looking directly at him.

Ron opened his mouth to speak, but Ed spoke up first. "Ladies and gentlemen. Sorry to be a little late, but we have something very exciting to talk about today. Ron, thanks for letting us refocus the agenda."

They weren't to follow the carved-in-stone agenda? Ron would have a stroke. Was Alex behind this mutiny? She shifted her gaze, to find him staring straight at her with all that blue-eyed intensity she knew so well. She dropped her gaze quickly. It hurt too much to look at him.

"We have a terrific new story line for Johnny," Ed went on. "One that's absolutely guaranteed to keep our ratings from plunging into the basement when Madeleine Marne finishes her stint with us next month."

This brought stirrings of interest from the vice presidents. Everyone around her sat up a little straighter. She slumped farther down in her seat. Their proposed story line was good, but not that good.

"And with us today to present his story line, is our new ..." Ed hesitated.

"Creative consultant," Fran whispered.

"Our new creative consultant, Alex MacHail."

She sat up straight and stared at Ed.

Ron leaned forward. "You mean to say Alex is contributing to his own story line?"

No one answered him. All the vice presidents looked at Alex.

Jo caught Ed's eye, but he sent her a bland look that gave nothing away. Fran wouldn't even meet her gaze. Didn't they have any concern at all for her feelings? Well, they wouldn't get away with this, the traitors. She folded her arms across her chest. Alex might be a talented actor, but he wasn't a writer.

Alex slowly rose to his feet and glanced around the table. He rubbed the palms of his hands together and cleared his throat. "My, uh, story line is about a guy who falls in love." He took a deep breath and blew out a puff of air.

She shifted around in her seat. How embarrassing. He hadn't even prepared a presentation. Did Ed and Fran plan on humiliating him in front of everyone? They should know she didn't want revenge. Alex wasn't Nick.

Alex rubbed the back of his neck. "That's sort of the classic story, I guess. But mine's a little different, because this guy was nearly crippled in an accident, and it gave him a whole new idea of what's important."

"That's good motivation," Ron said. "But we've done the nearly-crippled bit several times recently."

The gray-suited man seated next to Jo moved restlessly in his chair. Maybe Ron thought he was helping Alex out, but he was only making it worse.

Alex stared down at the conference table and didn't respond to Ron. "The only problem is that this guy goes after these new things in the same old way. He's always believed he could make things happen just because he wanted them so much. That works with his career—but it doesn't work with love."

He glanced sideways at Fran, who smiled and nodded encouragingly. Jo stared at Fran. Now she got it. He'd smooth-talked Fran and Ed into letting him plead his case with her. But what was the point? She already knew that he couldn't make himself love her. And he'd never convince her to agree to a one-sided marriage, not even for Buddy's sake.

"Okay, that's a good premise," Ron boomed, clearly trying to take back control of the meeting. "But we need more details about the actual story line."

Alex licked his lips and shot a look at Ed. "Right. The story line."

"Tell them about the kid," Ed prompted. "Johnny has a kid . . . you know."

"That's right. Johnny has a child, a son. But he doesn't tell Lorna about him until the little boy shows up one day." He lifted his gaze and met hers straight on. "Which is a big mistake."

"A kid," Ron interjected. "That's great. Kids are very big with the fans right now."

Alex kept on gazing straight at her. "He should have told her. But even though he loves her, loves her with everything he's got, he doesn't trust her. He can't trust anyone, because he still thinks he has to control everything himself."

She gripped the armrests of her chair. Could he be telling the truth? He sounded so desperate.

"He doesn't trust her to love him back in her own time and in her own way. Not only that, he can't trust his own child."

"That's not true," Jo couldn't help saying. She felt everyone's eyes shift to her. "He's a wonderful father."

"Have you been working on the script, too?" Ron asked from his end of the table.

"He can't let his son do anything," Alex countered.

"He's overprotective, sure, but it's still new to him. He'll get over it."

"He's scared all the time. What if something happened to his child? And there are so many things that can happen. Like the way he fell into the pool."

"A near drowning?" Ron asked. "We could use the old lakeside set for that."

Her gray-suited neighbor turned to Ron. "Will you stop interrupting?"

Alex flicked a grateful smile in Mr. Gray Suit's direction, then riveted Jo again with his gaze. "Do you think she'll ever forgive him for the things he said?"

"If he really does love her, she'll forgive him."

Alex paused. "He loves her." He moved along behind the others seated at the table. They twisted their heads around to see him. "He told her that already, but she didn't believe him."

Jo rose out of her chair and moved along her side of the table, parallel to Alex. "She believes him now."

"But does she love him?" Alex asked.

She met him at the end of the table, right behind Ron. "Yes, I do love you." She floated into his arms, and he kissed her and held her tight, as if he couldn't stop holding her, ever.

The room erupted with applause and loud whoops. Jo buried her face against Alex's shoulder. This was embarrassing—but worth it.

Alex pulled back a little to look at her. "Marry me?" he whispered. "I mean us—me and Buddy?"

"Yes, oh, yes," Jo whispered back.

Alex pulled her closer and kissed her again—a kiss of possession and of promise.

She heard Fran say, "I think we should give them some privacy, don't you?"

Over the sounds of people shuffling out of the room, Ron complained, "Will somebody please tell me what's going on?"

"The triumph of love, of course," Ed answered.

And Jo agreed wholeheartedly.

*   *   *   *   *

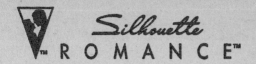

Silhouette
™ R O M A N C E™

COMING NEXT MONTH

#1090 THE DADDY LIST—Myrna Mackenzie
Fabulous Fathers
Faith Reynolds's little boy longed for a daddy—and she was determined to find him one. Then her son declared that handsome widower Nathan Murphy was his first choice. And Faith knew getting involved with Nathan could mean heartache.

#1091 THE BRIDAL SHOWER—Elizabeth August
Always a Bridesmaid
Emma Wynn was engaged to Mr. Almost-Right, but not if past love Mike Flint had anything to say about it. He was determined to find out if their shared passion was truly gone, or merely hidden deep within her....

#1092 RALEIGH AND THE RANCHER—Laura Anthony
Wranglers and Lace
Daniel McClintock couldn't deny his attraction to Raleigh, his pretty new ranch hand. But just when Daniel began to dream of their future, Raleigh's past threatened to drive her away. Would Daniel be able to show her how to trust in love again?

#1093 BACHELOR BLUES—Carolyn Zane
Confirmed bachelor Cole Richardson treasured his quiet home. Then Lark St. Clair and her mischievous daughter moved next door. Now he not only found himself losing his peace and quiet to this unpredictable pair, but also his heart!

#1094 STRANGER IN HER ARMS—Elizabeth Sites
Presumed dead, his estate dispersed, Alex returned from his ordeal in the Middle East determined to take back the family home...until he met Dominique Bellay, the lovely new owner. Now he wanted to start a new life with both!

#1095 WEDDING BELLS AND DIAPER PINS—Natalie Patrick
Debut Author
On her own, Dani McAdams couldn't win custody of her infant godson. So when ex-fiancé, Matt Taylor, offered a marriage of convenience her problems seemed to be solved. Until she discovered a passion for Matt that made her wish for something more.

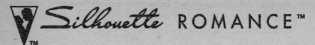

Silhouette ROMANCE™

is proud to present

The spirit of the West—and the magic of romance! Saddle up and get ready to fall in love Western-style with the third installment of WRANGLERS AND LACE. Coming in July with:

Raleigh and the Rancher
by Laura Anthony

Raleigh Travers was wary of love; she had enough on her mind working the ranch and raising her young brother. So when she sensed romantic feelings for rugged Daniel McClintock, the ranch owner, she was careful to keep them to herself. But Raleigh didn't bet on Daniel returning those feelings, or being as bullheaded as a runaway steer in forcing her to acknowledge their passion.

Wranglers and Lace: Hard to tame—impossible to resist—these cowboys meet their match.

SL-3

He's Too Hot To Handle...but she can take a little heat.

SILHOUETTE

Summer Sizzlers

This summer don't be left in the cold, join Silhouette for the hottest Summer Sizzlers collection. The perfect summer read, on the beach or while vacationing, Summer Sizzlers features sexy heroes who are "Too Hot To Handle." This collection of three new stories is written by bestselling authors Mary Lynn Baxter, Ann Major and Laura Parker.

Available this July wherever Silhouette books are sold.

SS95

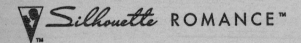

HE'S MORE THAN A MAN,
HE'S ONE OF OUR

THE DADDY LIST
Myrna Mackenzie

When beautiful Faith Reynolds and her little boy, Cory, came into the picture, Nathan Murphy couldn't resist becoming a part of their life. Nathan's unhappy past made him sure he'd never be a family man again. But how could he leave Faith and Cory without hurting them...or himself?

Look for *The Daddy List* by Myrna Mackenzie, available in July.

Fall in love with our Fabulous Fathers!

ROMANCE™

FF795

ANNOUNCING THE

PRIZE SURPRISE SWEEPSTAKES!

This month's prize:

L-A-R-G-E—SCREEN PANASONIC TV!

This month, as a special surprise, we're giving away a fabulous FREE TV!

Imagine how delighted you and your family will be to own this brand-new 31" Panasonic** television! It comes with all the latest high-tech features, like a SuperFlat picture tube for a clear, crisp picture...unified remote control...closed-caption decoder...clock and sleep timer, and much more!

The facing page contains two Entry Coupons (as does every book you received this shipment). Complete and return *all* the entry coupons; **the more times you enter, the better your chances of winning the TV!**

Then keep your fingers crossed, because you'll find out by July 15, 1995 if you're the winner!

Remember: The more times you enter, the better your chances of winning!*

PTV KAL

PRIZE SURPRISE
SWEEPSTAKES
OFFICIAL ENTRY COUPON

This entry must be received by: JUNE 30, 1995
This month's winner will be notified by: JULY 15, 1995

YES, I want to win the Panasonic 31" TV! Please enter me in the drawing and let me know if I've won!

Name_____

Address _____ Apt. _____

City	State/Prov.	Zip/Postal Code

Account #_____

Return entry with invoice in reply envelope.

CTV KAL

PRIZE SURPRISE
SWEEPSTAKES
OFFICIAL ENTRY COUPON

This entry must be received by: JUNE 30, 1995
This month's winner will be notified by: JULY 15, 1995

YES, I want to win the Panasonic 31" TV! Please enter me in the drawing and let me know if I've won!

Name_____

Address _____ Apt. _____

City	State/Prov.	Zip/Postal Code

Account #_____

Return entry with invoice in reply envelope.

© 1995 HARLEQUIN ENTERPRISES LTD.   CTV KAL